DATE DUE

JUN. 3 1983	JAN 2 5	
JUN. 1 8 1988	JUN. 2 2 1992	
JUN. 2 4 1988	JUN. 1 1 1994	
DEC 21 1983	JUN 21 2006	
DEC 3 1984	JUN 2 6 2006	
MAY 21 1986		
FEB 20 1987		
FEB 1 0 1988		
JAN 2		

The Evidence
That Wasn't There

Also by C.S. Adler
The Cat That Was Left Behind

C.S. Adler

THE EVIDENCE THAT WASN'T THERE

CLARION BOOKS
TICKNOR & FIELDS: A HOUGHTON MIFFLIN COMPANY
NEW YORK

With thanks for the helpful information provided by:
Sergeant Darryl Ostrander and Sergeant Dan Pasquariello
of the Niskayuna Police Department
Also, Norman E. Robbins
of the U.S. Postal Inspection Service

CLARION BOOKS
Ticknor & Fields, a Houghton Mifflin Company

Library of Congress Cataloging in Publication Data
Adler, C. S.   The evidence that wasn't there.
Summary: Kim must move fast to keep a favorite teacher
from getting involved with a mysterious con-artist,
and to save her own life.
[1. Mystery and detective stories.
2. Swindlers and swindling—Fiction]   I. Title.
PZ7.A26145Ev   [Fic]   82-1194
ISBN 0-89919-117-7   AACR2

*Books are like ships that need good pilots
to bring them to port.
Thanks to Jim Giblin for piloting
my Clarion books so well.*

chapter one

I had reason not to like him when I met him, bumped into him to be exact, but I wasn't scared of him at first. None of what happened between us would have started, either, if only Mother hadn't been called to cover the faculty members' art show that Saturday. That left me alone in the apartment, disappointed because I'd been looking forward to a mother-daughter shopping trip.

After a couple of hours of sitting in the bathtub playing my flute to keep myself company, the water cooled and I got lonely. The one place I knew I'd find companionship was Ms. Davis's house, so I hauled myself out of the tub and ten minutes later was whipping out of our garden apartment complex on my bike, heading down Van Worth Road toward trouble.

Ms. Davis is my English teacher in high school, honors English. I'm only in it because I try hard, and my freshman year teacher liked me. Ms. Davis and I became friends when I stayed late to help her count books one afternoon. She rescued me from the pouring rain by offering me a lift home. En route we discovered we lived near each other and shared what she called "a romantic view of life." I liked that. It made me feel appealing.

Ms. Davis lives with her mother in an old fashioned cottage crouched under the branches of enormous maple trees. Her driveway was littered with huge, scarlet-fingered leaves. I noticed a man in a business suit, carrying an attaché case, leaving the house. Then the wind slapped a hand-sized leaf across my face, startling me so I swerved my bike and caromed right into him. His attaché case whacked against a tree and flipped open. The wind took off with all the papers inside it, tossing them about recklessly.

"I'm so sorry!" I cried and immediately dropped my bike and began scrambling after papers, scooping them up and stuffing them back into his case.

"Don't touch those," the man snapped and grabbed documents from my hands as if he thought I, and not the wind, was the thief.

"I'm just trying to help," I said. "I'm really sorry. It was an accident. The wind—"

"Nothing ever goes right for me, nothing," he mumbled, ignoring me as he scuttled about after his belongings.

"Here you are," I said, plucking something that looked like a fold out of a family tree from a barberry bush.

"What are you doing here?" He straightened up and glared at me.

"I'm coming to visit the Davises."

"What for?"

"I'm a friend of theirs," I said, surprised by his question.

His face went through an odd transformation as he thought that one over. The eyes that looked like blue chips lost some of their hardness, and the mouth that was just an angry line emerged into lips. All of a sudden he looked like an eager-to-please, nondescript salesman in his late twenties, early thirties, whereas before he'd struck me as a pretty nasty character. "Just coming by for a visit?" he asked.

"Yes. I'm sorry," I said again, gesturing at the papers.

He nodded. "Well, help me then. These are irreplaceable papers, absolutely irreplaceable. I need them for my business, you understand?"

"Sure," I said, and for the next ten minutes we scrambled about the yard and street until everything had been picked up. I unwrapped the page of D's from a telephone book, that was clinging to my hockey-stick-thin legs, and handed that to him silently, not knowing if it was his or not—but he accepted it.

Tearing pages from telephone books seemed strange to me, and so did the assortment of papers I'd collected for him. I wondered what his business was. His stock of calling cards indicated he was a genealogist. That was somebody who found out who your ancestors were, which accounted for all the family trees. Then there had been data sheets and newspaper clippings and letters and a diploma from some college and a license with a seal stamped on it from the state of Virginia.

"I guess that's it," I said.

"All right. . . . You didn't keep anything, did you?"

"Me? Of course not."

"No." He nodded vaguely and, without thanking me, began looking around again. I stowed my bike alongside the Davises' garage out of sight of the street and rang the doorbell, leaving him to his anxious searching.

Emma answered. She's Ms. Davis's mother. Emma has bifocals, perfect white curls, and is built of cushions of varying size from her cheeks down to her small, plump feet. She's my substitute grandma, the only one I've ever known, and I love her even though she does have a myopic view of life and never stops talking.

"Deirdre's at a meeting, Kim," Emma said. "But you come in and wait for her. I have the most exciting news. Would you believe Deirdre and me might be heirs to a fortune? Isn't that something?" She hugged me out of sheer delight. I hugged her back. Emma's eminently huggable.

"You're kidding, aren't you? A fortune? How did you hear?"

4

"I shouldn't tell you. He said not to say a word to anybody, and we don't even know if we're the right Davises yet, but I'm so excited I have to tell somebody, and you can keep a secret, can't you, Kim?"

"Sure," I said. Whoever says no to that question?

"Well, come out to the kitchen then," Emma said. She ushered me through the living room stuffed with upholstered chairs full of fringes and lamps with frilly shades—Emma's kind of room, not Ms. Davis at all. In the kitchen she sat me down at the table in front of a plate of butterscotch brownies and poured me a glass of milk, too busy talking to ask if I wanted it or not.

"Wouldn't it be something if he turned out to be a distant relative? Thirty-second cousin or something. I like that young man. He did say I remind him of his dear departed mother. Oh, how he loved his mother! His eyes just lit right up when he mentioned her name."

"What young man? Who are you talking about now, Emma?"

"Who? Why the young man who was just here. Malcolm Davis Orlop. Isn't that an elegant name? Suits him to a T. Such lovely manners. He—"

"You mean the sandy haired guy with the receding hairline I met coming in? *That's* who you're talking about?"

"Oh, you met Malcolm? Yes." Emma went babbling on about the fortune she was to inherit, but

5

I'd stopped listening. I had to try and reconcile Emma's and my impressions of the man I'd bumped into. When I tuned in again, I asked a few questions.

A lot of Emma's answers were confusing, but this is what I managed to understand. Somewhere in Texas a wealthy man named Percy Lambreth Davis, who owned part interest in half the industries in the state, had died without leaving a will. His wife claimed and received half of his money, but his brothers had rights to the rest. However, they were all either dead or had disappeared.

According to Orlop, any surviving cousins, or even their children, had a right to lay claim to the half billion of remaining assets. What Orlop was doing was tracking down all the heirs so they could register as claimants and band together to sue for their share in the estate.

When I asked Emma why they needed to sue if they were rightful heirs, she said Orlop told her the industries and banks were trying to hide the money Percy Lambreth Davis had in their companies because they wanted it for themselves. "Hanky panky" was Emma's term for it.

"You mean Orlop thinks the big businesses and banks are trying to rip off the heirs, Emma?" I asked.

"Yes, that's it."

"But what does Mr. Orlop get out of all this?"

"Why, he stands to inherit, too, through his

mother's side, but of course it would cost too much for him to fight this thing by himself. Malcolm says if we each pitch in some money, though, we can be strong enough to do it together. Just like little David slew Goliath, Malcolm says."

"And you're sure this Percy Lambreth Davis is a relative of yours?"

"Well, that's what Malcolm's going to check out first. It's my late husband's family, of course. But Malcolm says he's pretty sure we're related, according to what I told him."

I certainly hoped Ms. Davis was going to inherit a lot of money. From what she and Emma had let slip, I knew they were snowed under by debts. Over the years Emma had had every major operation imaginable, gall bladder and hip and back and heart, and between that and furnace and roof and Ms. Davis's deadbeat car always needing to be repaired, they really were in sad straits. That wasn't what Emma told me she wanted the money for, though. She wanted it so Ms. Davis could fulfill her dream of a trip to Greece.

"The poor girl never gets anything," Emma said. "Not since her father died and left me on her hands with all these ailments. Of course Deirdre would never complain, but she deserves something for herself for a change."

Ms. Davis called about then to say she was going from the meeting to a friend's house for lunch. Soon after, I said good-bye to Emma. As I collected my bike from behind the brush where I'd left it, I saw something small and white. It was one of his calling cards. Malcolm Davis Orlop, Licensed Genealogist, State of Virginia. I slipped it into my jacket pocket, mounted my bike, and was on my way home when I saw Orlop get out his car and wave at me to stop. Instead, I stood up on my pedals and poured on the speed to get away from him. True, he wore a business suit and looked ordinary, but I remembered his face all cross-stitched with anger at me. No way did I want anything more to do with that man.

Back home, I lugged my bike inside, shut the downstairs door, ran upstairs and locked the inside door to our apartment behind me, too, for good measure.

When I slid open the door to our three-by-six-foot balcony, I could hear the sounds of disco music coming from the apartment downstairs. That meant Mother's friend Jo Ann was home. Good. Knowing she was there was enough; I didn't need to visit her. I'm not especially enthused about Jo Ann—all she talks about is the way men have taken advantage of her.

The phone rang. "Kim, it's Emma. What did you do to Malcolm Orlop this morning?"

"I didn't do anything."

"Well, he came by right after you left. He says he has to see you about something, but I wouldn't give him your address. I didn't think that was proper. I did say I'd ask you to drop by here after lunch tomorrow when he comes back with those documents. That's all right, isn't it?"

"Did he say what he wants to see me about?"

"No, dear."

I didn't like it. I didn't like the sound of it at all. "O.K., Emma," I said reluctantly. "I'll try to come." I wished my mother would hurry home. I wanted protection. The image of Orlop's blue chip eyes and twisted lips made me nervous.

chapter two

A dream about Orlop pursuing me woke me up on Sunday morning. I padded out to the kitchen and saw it was only eight o'clock. Mother was still sound asleep. Through her open bedroom door, I could hear her snoring lightly. Sleep had taken away the careworn lines from her plump face and she looked pretty.

Mother had been so frazzled from all the foul-ups at the faculty members' art show yesterday that I hadn't had the heart to tell her about Orlop. She worried enough about having to leave me alone so much, as it was. The problem is Mom lets her boss take advantage of her because she's afraid of losing her job. She thinks she's lucky to be a publicity person when the only job she ever had before the divorce was as a secretary.

The smell of the cinnamon on the French toast I was making us for breakfast brought Mother into the kitchen sniffing.

"Yum, ambrosia. Aren't you a marvelous child!"

"Be ready in a minute, Ma. What're your plans for the day?"

"First I'll soak my undernourished brain in the *Sunday Times*. Then maybe later in the afternoon, we can take a hike through the nature park. Would you like that?"

"Fine," I said. "This morning I'm off to the drugstore to get a birthday card."

"Oh," she said with a pained look, "it's your father's birthday, isn't it."

I nodded. "This year you didn't have to remind me for a change," I said. It was funny the way she encouraged me to do all the daughterly things I could do long distance, like send cards and letters. But she did it grudgingly, as if she didn't think he deserved attention.

"I might stop in at the Davises on my way back from the store," I said.

"Enjoy," she said. "I'll look for you around lunchtime."

Picking a birthday card for my father didn't take very long. I chose one with a picture of the moon over the sea and neutral wording. Since he'd moved to California with his second wife and their children, our main contact has been birthday cards and Christmas presents. Every so often I write him a letter to keep him current with my growth and development, and he always answers. I hope he understands my letters better than I do his. Mostly he seems to talk in circles without saying much. Mother says that's the way he is. It took her two days to figure out what he wanted when he asked her for the divorce five years ago.

Mother says she's probably a better person without him now that the shock of being deserted has worn off and she's built a new life for herself and me. I guess I'm better off too. My only complaint is she spends so much time and energy on her job, either working late or going out of town or bringing work home, that she has very little left. Lots of times I end up keeping problems to myself rather than burdening her with them. I used to have my best friend, Francine, to confide in, but she's off in Washington, D.C. this year. Her father got some kind of grant.

Walking back from the drugstore, I saw Morey Stern mowing the Davises' side lawn. Morey does all the Davises' odd jobs. Ms. Davis is a real fan of his. She says Morey has more ability packed into every solid inch of him than any other kid in the high school. She may be right.

I guess I take Morey for granted from having spent all those predawn hours riding the band bus with him. That was before he gave up lugging the cello, which was nearly as big as he is, and got into reviving the high school literary magazine. Morey's funny and good humored and everybody likes him. I do, too, even if he does only come up to my chin.

I was waving at Morey, trying to get his attention over the noise of the lawnmower, when Malcolm

Davis Orlop walked out of the Davises' house toward me. Emma had said "afternoon" and it was still morning. Before I could even consider trying to get away, Orlop took hold of my arm and got right to the point.

"I believe you found something of mine yesterday."

"What?" I asked.

"You know what. I'm surprised at you. Mrs. Davis says you're such a nice girl. Nice girls don't keep things that don't belong to them." A muscle worked in his jaw and his lips disappeared into a thin line again.

"I don't know what you're talking about, Mr. Orlop. Will you let go of me, please?" I tried to pull out of his grasp, but I couldn't. He stood there frowning at me as if I'd done something terrible to him.

"You took it," he said. "Don't deny you took it. I saw you."

"Took what?"

"There's nothing in it that you can use. It's important only to me. It's my private business, understand?"

"I really don't have anything of yours."

He looked as if he didn't believe me. "Stop stalling. You're not fooling me."

"I wouldn't take anything of yours," I said. "Why should I?"

"To spite me maybe. To get me in trouble."

"How could I get you in trouble?"

Something was, as Morey would say, definitely not kosher. Orlop scared me, and he was holding me so hard it hurt. "Where do you have it?" he demanded. "Where did you put it?"

"I don't *have* anything of yours!" I struggled to get my arm free. Maybe my fear made me remember the calling card that I'd stuffed in my jacket pocket. "You mean when I picked up my bike? That?" I asked.

"That's exactly what I mean," he said grimly.

"Well, if that's all you want," I said, "let go of me. I'd be happy to return that card to you. It's in my other jacket at home."

"Get in my car. I'll drive you."

"No way will I get in your car."

"Why not?"

"Because one of the first things my mother ever taught me was not to get in cars with strangers." I said that with a little smile, but Orlop didn't smile back.

"I'm not a stranger. You know who I am."

"You wait here," I said. "And I'll bring you what you want."

"You're making me mad," he said. "I don't like sneaky kids like you who think you're so smart. You get in my car now."

"Morey!" I yelled in desperation. The lawnmower had stopped some time ago.

14

"What's the matter, Kim?" Morey came across the yard at a run as if he'd been observing what was going on and was waiting for his cue.

Orlop dropped my arm. "Morey, this man—" I said, rubbing the forearm where he'd gripped me.

"It's all right," Orlop hastened to say. "You run home and get it, and I'll wait here for you like you said. It's all right if that's the way you want to do it. So long as you give back what's mine."

I took an uncertain breath, glad that Morey was standing there like a short, black-browed bull ready to charge. At least I had someone on my side. "OK, I'll be right back." I turned to Morey and explained. "I have something that belongs to Mr. Orlop. I'm going to run home and get it. Will you be around here for a while?"

He got the message. Trust Morey to pick up on a hint. "Sure," he said. "I'll still be here when you get back."

I jogged home worrying. The whole business didn't make sense to me. What was so important about a calling card? People had them printed up just so they could hand them out. Mother had left a note for me on the apartment door. She was downstairs having coffee with Jo Ann. I got the card from my jacket pocket and looked it over. Nothing. Not even an address or a telephone number.

Orlop was sitting in his car waiting for me when I returned on my bike. I handed him the card through the open window. "Here you are," I said.

He took it and turned it over in his hand as if it puzzled him. "Where's the letter?" he asked.

"What letter?"

"Let me tell you, kid, it's not smart to hide that letter on me, not smart at all. You give me back that letter—or else."

I backed away from that twitching face with the stone chip eyes focused on me as if they'd like to cut me to pieces.

"What's up now, Kim?" Morey asked appearing at my side. I reached out a trembling hand just to touch his warm flesh for comfort. "This guy giving you a hard time?" Morey asked.

"Not me," Orlop said and revved his engine. "I'm not doing anything to her. She's the one. Little troublemaker. You better remember what I said, girl." He jerked into drive and took off fast.

I stood there shuddering in the middle of the street, paying no attention to the cars that swerved wide to get around me. Morey took my bike and led me out of the street onto the Davises' lawn. "What a weird guy. What'd he want from you?"

"I don't know." I bit my lip. "He's so mad at me! He thinks I've got a letter of his and I don't. How do I give him back something that I don't even have?" If I sounded tearful, that's because I was on the verge of bawling.

Morey made me sit down on the grass and explain the whole story to him. His intelligent, dark brown eyes were so full of sympathy that it was a relief just to have him listening to me.

"Do you think Orlop's pulling some kind of con job on Emma?" Morey asked me when I'd finished.

"You mean about the inheritance? I don't know. He *could* be a crook. Maybe that's why he's so nervous."

"Did he get any money from Emma?"

"She didn't say he'd asked her for any. Just that he wanted her to register or something." I remembered the whole inheritance possibility was supposed to be a big secret. "Morey, I promised I wouldn't tell anybody. I don't want the Davises to lose out on anything if—"

"Don't worry about it. I'm not going to tell anybody anything unless there's reason to believe Orlop's a swindler. Let's find out if Emma's given him any money. If she has, I think we ought to go tell the police."

"The police?"

"Look, he threatened you, didn't he?"

"Well, he was mad because—yes, I guess he did threaten me."

"That's got to be against the law. Come on. We'll talk to Emma."

Morey's not only a brain, he also acts fast. That's probably how he manages to run the literary magazine and still play volleyball and bring home pockets full of A's in honors courses. He has so much energy he makes everybody else seem anemic, especially me. I have trouble even getting myself out of bed and off to school most mornings, and I'm happiest just lying around listening to music or playing my flute or having long conversations with people I care about. Morey's happiest in rapid motion.

Within fifteen minutes, he had stowed the lawn mower in the garage, convinced Emma we wouldn't starve without an infusion of milk and cookies, and found out that Orlop had just shown Emma an article from a newspaper telling about the unclaimed assets of the Percy Lambreth Davis estate. "The newspaper said there might be a billion dollars. That's a lot of money, a billion dollars."

"And newspapers don't lie, do they?" Morey said.

"No, they don't."

"Even when they say 'might' be?"

"Morey Stern, you're talking fresh to me. I know that article isn't proof enough. That's why Malcolm's going to bring me more before I—"

"Before you what?"

"I'm not talking. And Kim, I must say, I'm surprised at you. You promised me you wouldn't tell a soul, and here you get Morey involved as if it was his business."

"But, Emma," I protested. "Mr. Orlop *threatened* me. He thinks I have some letter or something I really don't have."

"Seems to me he has good reason to be suspicious. First you knock the poor man down, and then you take something that belongs to him and hide it."

"Emma, I didn't! All I took was one of his cards. That doesn't count for anything. They're made to hand out to people." I was hurt. How could she turn on me like this after months of feeding me full of cookies and cake? How could she trust some man who happened into her life to offer her a few million dollars over me?

"Did your husband ever mention having any rich relatives?" Morey asked, back to his investigation.

"Now Morey, this is none of your business. It really isn't," Emma said.

"But did he?"

"Well, Mr. Davis was never one to do much talking about his family. He didn't have much use for his family. There were some well-to-do relatives out in Ohio that he didn't like at all."

"Ohio isn't Texas," Morey said. "And well-to-do doesn't sound like half a billion dollars."

"People move all the time," Emma said sharply. "What you don't appreciate is that Malcolm is investing all his time and his own money in this. It's like a—a crusade for him. And he's not a healthy person. He has a nervous stomach and can't eat just anything, and restaurant food is so bad for him. But instead of taking care of himself, he's out to help people like Deirdre and me."

"You would admit, though, that you never heard

19

of Percy Lambreth Davis before Orlop mentioned him to you?" Morey persisted.

"That doesn't mean he wasn't a relative," Emma said, setting her lips stubbornly.

"I guess he must have shown you something besides the newspaper article, though," Morey said.

"Certainly. I saw several letters from very important people. Like a bank president named Davis and a senator. Oh, lots of people are registering as heirs. Some have even gotten money already. You know, Morey, I wasn't born yesterday."

"I know, Emma. I'd just hate to see the best cookie baker in the whole town taken in by a con man."

Emma sniffed, less impressed by the flattery than the criticism of her hero. "Malcolm Davis Orlop is not a con man," she informed Morey. "He's neat and clean and polite, and he shows respect for his elders. Why, I never heard a grown man speak more lovingly about his mother. He still misses her something terrible and she's been gone two years. Do you know he never married because he was too busy taking care of her? She was widowed young. They even had some kind of business together. He says she taught him all he knows. Oh, don't tell me anything could be bad about that man. I'm a good judge of character if I say so myself, and I say Malcolm's a gentleman down to his toes."

Emma's defense of Malcolm Orlop hadn't won either Morey or me over, but before we could counterattack, Ms. Davis called from upstairs. She wanted Emma to make out a check to Elwood's garage. Her friend Dale was going to drive her over there so Ms. Davis could retrieve her car, which had just been repaired.

Emma didn't budge. She pursed her lips and her eyes skipped guiltily back and forth between Morey and me. Then Ms. Davis appeared in the doorway to the living room, her frizzy hair in its usual uproar. Ms. Davis is not pretty. Her features squeeze together in the center of her face, and one eye tends to wander, but today she looked cute in jeans and a plaid shirt.

"Hi, kids. I didn't know you were here. Kim, I'm sorry I missed you yesterday. How about coming by later today?"

"Can't," I said. "Mother and I are going on a hike."

"Well, soon then."

"I will," I said.

"You go to Elwood's too, Ms. Davis?" Morey said. "My dad says he's the best mechanic around."

"Oh, Frank's my buddy. He claims I kept him from flunking English and dropping out of school. Emma, the check, please. Dale's going to honk for me any minute. I've got to rush, kids. I'm sorry."

"The thing is, Deirdre," Emma interrupted. "It slipped my mind you planned to pick up your car today. I can write you a check, but there isn't enough in the account to cover it."

"There isn't? I thought you said you had scraped together a few hundred."

Emma sounded so guilty as she babbled vaguely about other bills that had come up that I had immediate suspicions about where the few hundred had gone.

"Can you put Frank Elwood off for a while?" she asked finally.

"I hate to do that," Ms. Davis said. "He's already doing me a favor getting the car repaired so fast and reasonably."

Emma looked crushed.

"Oh, Mother, don't feel bad," Ms. Davis said. "It's not your fault. Look, if we don't have it, he'll just have to wait. I'll go ahead with Dale and tell him to hang in there. Frank will understand."

"Soon you'll have all the money you need for everything, Deirdre."

Ms. Davis laughed. "You mean that marvelous inheritance your friend Orlop talks about? Don't let him get your hopes too high. You know Papa would never have let us forget it if we were related to a man that rich. There's a million Davises in the world. Mr. Orlop's probably got us confused with another family."

"Is that what you think?" Emma said. "Well, you just wait and see. I think you're going to be pleasantly surprised, Deirdre. You mark my words."

Two short toots and a long one summoned Ms.

Davis. She grabbed a sweater from the coat closet and ran outside. After she'd gone, Morey asked, "What did Orlop need the money for, Emma?"

"Why, for registering the claim. I only gave him a hundred and fifty dollars. The rest I'll give him later after—" She crimped her lips together, realizing she'd let Morey trick her into that admission.

I felt sorry for Emma. So did Morey. He started talking about the lawn and his plans for getting their leaves raked up. Then when he had her perked up again, he eased the two of us out of the house.

"I'm not surprised that she told Ms. Davis, even though she said she wasn't going to," I said to Morey outside. "Emma couldn't keep a secret to save her life." I smiled.

"It's not funny," Morey said.

"What's not funny?"

"None of it. Come on. We're going to the police."

"What for? What can we tell them?"

"That Emma gave that guy a hundred and fifty dollars for what is probably a nonexistent inheritance, and that she's planning to give him more money when he comes back."

"But Morey, maybe she's right. Maybe it's not nonexistent. If he brings proof—"

"What kind of proof? Phony letters? Phony documents? You think Emma's capable of judging how authentic something is? She's going to accept anything that looks half-kosher. Besides, even if the whole thing is legitimate—he still threatened you. Let's go report him."

Morey pedaled his bike standing up the whole way to the police station while I trailed behind him. I was thinking that even though Morey wasn't a close friend like Francine, I could count on him at least. My dream man, Eric, the basketball star in my math class, probably wouldn't even notice if I got kidnapped under his nose.

I wished that Morey weren't so short. It would be lovely to have a crush on a boy like him instead of one like Eric who didn't even know I existed.

Chapter three

Morey locked our bikes onto a lamppost in the rear of the new brick town offices building where the police station was now located. I'd never even been in a police station, but with Morey in the lead, I was ready to march anywhere. A curly haired young officer whose name tag said Sergeant Morton asked us what our business was.

"We think we're onto a swindler," Morey announced.

Sergeant Morton grinned. "You are, huh? Well, is it an emergency? Someone in the act of committing a crime?"

"Not exactly. Although in a way— See, this guy is taking an old lady's money, claiming she's heir to a fortune. Also, he threatened Kim."

"Oh, yeah?" Sergeant Morton raised his skimpy eyebrows until they disappeared into his thatched hair. "Are you over sixteen, Kim?" he asked me.

"No."

"Then you'd better get an adult like your mother or father and come back and we'll take your supporting deposition."

"But I don't want to tell my mother. She'd worry herself sick. Can't you just let us tell you what happened?"

"Sure, I can let you tell me, but if we're going to charge this guy with anything, we need an adult to cosign your deposition. That's the way the law reads."

"How about if I bring my father?" Morey said. "He'd come."

"Are you the party bringing the charge?"

"No, I'm the witness."

"No good. If she's bringing the charge, she's gotta bring the adult."

I groaned.

"Look," Sergeant Morton said helpfully. "Why don't you come into my office and tell me about it unofficially. Maybe we got something here and maybe we don't."

He led us down the corridor lined with open office doors to a room with a big metal table. Morey and I sat down on one side and Sergeant Morton sat on the other. He wrote down our names and addresses and asked us a lot of questions that seemed irrelevant to me. Finally he got to the point. "First of all, Kim, what did he threaten you with?"

"His voice."

"No, I mean what did he say?"

"He said I'd better give him back the letter or else."

"Where's the letter?"

"I don't know. I never even saw a letter—I mean, not his."

"Did he physically abuse you in any way?"

"Well, he grabbed my arm."

"Leave any marks?"

I pushed up the sleeve of my sweater to show him. We all stared at my arm. Nothing there.

"See, if you wanted to charge him with assault," Sergeant Morton explained patiently, "you'd need evidence of physical injury. Just grabbing an arm is harassment."

"What would he get on harassment?" Morey asked.

"Nothing much. Harassment's only a violation; it's not considered a crime. At the most, a two hundred and fifty dollar fine or fifteen days, something like that—if he got convicted, that is. It's not likely he'd be convicted unless the victim had some bruises or lacerations or something."

"And threatening me?"

"Same thing, just harassment. Of course, you can sign an accusatory instrument in the presence of an adult, and present it to a judge. He'll issue a warrant for the subject's arrest if he thinks there's enough to go on."

"But it's still just a violation?" Morey asked.

"That's all it is. What else you got?"

"What else?" I asked.

"In the way of evidence."

"Well, what about fraud?" Morey asked. "He took a hundred and fifty dollars from Mrs. Davis and he's coming back for more."

"What did he say the hundred and fifty was for?"

"Registering her claim to the inheritance."

"No," the sergeant said. "You don't have to register to inherit anything. No law in this state says you have to register. What's the rest of the money for?"

"We don't know."

"Yeah, well, fraud is more serious business. Now, if we were investigating him for fraud, this Mrs. Davis would have to come in, or somebody else he contacted, and sign a deposition, and then we'd investigate. You know, check to see if the guy has a record, find out if there is such an estate. But you'd need some solid evidence, and in any case, you'd have to get Mrs. Davis, or whoever's been contacted, to come in and complain. We just don't have the time or the manpower to go running off checking out everybody's suspicions without something to go on."

"But if Kim does bring her mother in, then what?" Morey asked.

"Then we summon him to appear in court. Could take a long time, and at best—and I don't even say you've got a case—he could get a fine or a couple of days in jail. It's not going to interfere with his operation much if he's committing a fraud. He'll come right out of jail and finish up the job. See what I mean? If you want to nail him on fraud, it's better to hold the harassment charge in abeyance or you'll blow your chances to get the evidence you need."

Morey and I sat there in glum silence for a minute. Finally Sergeant Morton said to me, "If you're worried he might hassle you some more, we could keep an eye on your apartment, but that's about it unless he does something that breaks the law."

"Like knife somebody or beat somebody up?" Morey said.

"Yeah, or breaking and entering," Sergeant Morton said, refusing to bite on the sarcasm. "See, we can't get him for intending to commit a crime, only for what he's done if his victim is willing to accuse him of it."

"So I have to wait to be beaten up or killed?" I asked in disbelief.

"We'll try to prevent that happening," the sergeant said with a smile. "You'd better stay close to home. Don't go anywhere alone. Stick with your friends or parents for a while."

Another policeman came to the door and asked to see the sergeant about something urgent. I stood up, ready to go. It seemed pretty clear to me that the police were too bound up in rules and regulations to be much help. Morey gestured me back in my seat. "I'm not done yet," he said, and when Sergeant Morton finally returned to us, Morey asked

29

him, "What are you going to do about Mrs. Davis's money?"

The sergeant shook his head regretfully. "Fraud is hard to prove, unless the guy uses the mail. Then you can go to the U.S. Postal Inspection Service. They'll investigate any complaint where the U.S. mail is being used in a scheme to defraud, and of course, they're federal. If he's operating in more than one place, which is usual, the Service can really get it all together and make a case out of it. He could get put away for ten, twenty years."

"But he's not mailing anything. He rips pages out of phone books and drives right up to people's doors to take their money," I said, remembering the D's page wrapped around my leg.

"Yeah, well, like I said, your Mrs. Davis would have to file a complaint."

"Mrs. Davis will never believe anything bad about Orlop."

"There you are!" Sergeant Morton shrugged. "We'll keep an eye on your apartment, though."

"What does that mean exactly?" Morey asked.

"Oh, that we'll stop off and check on our usual patrols."

Morey frowned. "Suppose Orlop drops by to hassle Kim when you're not driving past?"

"Then she calls us. Look, kid—" he was still being patient—"I don't make the rules here. I'm just supposed to catch people when they break the law."

30

We thanked the sergeant and left. I felt worse than when we'd gone in. "It's hopeless," I said to Morey.

"You know something?" Morey said. "That letter Orlop thinks you have must be evidence against him. Maybe he knows about the U.S. Postal Inspection Service. Otherwise, why would he get so shook up about your having his letter?"

"I *don't* have it."

"Yeah, but neither does he, right?"

"So?"

"So, maybe it'll turn up. In the meantime, don't you go anywhere alone, and we'll keep after Emma. Maybe she'll get suspicious enough so we can talk her into filing a complaint against Orlop."

"You can't convince Emma of anything she doesn't already know," I said with a sigh. "Even Ms. Davis can't."

"Kim, you live alone with your mother, don't you?" Morey asked.

"Yes. And she's out a lot at night. Sometimes she even goes away on business trips for a couple of days." I was feeling quivery just thinking about that.

"You could move in with us if she has to go anywhere," Morey said cheerfully. "My grandparents are living with us now. That makes six of us all talking at once. My mother would never notice another person in all that noise. You'd have to sleep with my little sister, though, and I have to warn you—she bites."

31

"You're a doll, Morey." I smiled at him.

"I mean it, Kim. All you have to do is call me. We always have room for one more."

On impulse I bent and kissed one of his wild black eyebrows. "Thanks anyway," I said.

"Anytime. I like the way you show your gratitude."

He escorted me home and left me at the door to my apartment. I ran upstairs thinking that the only good thing that had come out of the day was I'd learned to appreciate Morey more. He was a real friend, and I could certainly use another friend. Orlop's "or else" was running like a broken record in my head.

chapter four

Before he left me at my apartment, Morey had suggested that I try talking to Ms. Davis about Orlop and our suspicions. "Maybe *she* can do something with her mother," Morey said. So even though I was supposed to go to a special orchestra rehearsal right after school on Monday, I skipped it and headed toward the Davises instead.

I pedaled fast to keep warm in the cold wind. It smelled like winter although the red and gold leaves were still bright as stained glass in the sunlight. To keep my mind off my troubles, I had a daydream going about Eric. The leaves were in the daydream too. Eric and I were walking through the woods hand in hand while yellow leaves sifted over his golden head and his enigmatic, Genghis Khan eyes stared down at me. In school Eric passes silently among the rest of us mortals, mysteriously apart, all bony, six foot five of him. I never dare say a word to him in school. I just look. But in the dream I asked, "What are you thinking about, Eric?"

"You," he answered. "I think about you all the time."

Isn't it wonderful the miracles daydreams produce? Ms. Davis says daydreams are the seeds of art. She often says things like that. She's probably the best English teacher I will ever have in my life even if the principal is always after her for getting her records and clerical forms messed up. When she reads aloud to our class, shivers go down my spine. It's that beautiful. And she gets us to write things we'd never let any other teacher see. Ms. Davis makes us feel smarter and better than we really are.

Emma was cool when she let me in, still mad at me because I'd suspected her hero of "hanky panky," I guess.

"It's Kim," Emma yelled down the hall. "Are you busy, Deirdre?"

"Kim! Come on in my office," Ms. Davis called, and I went.

Ms. Davis's study is off limits to Emma. It's the one room in the house that Ms. Davis can be private in. She's got it furnished Ms. Davis style with a beanbag chair, which I always fold myself into, and a secondhand executive desk and chair that she says makes her feel efficient. Books are squeezed in every which way on bookcases stacked with student folders and papers. Only the sketches of Greece on the walls are orderly. Greece is Ms. Davis's dream the way Eric is mine.

"Isn't it glorious outside, Kim?" Ms. Davis asked.

"The colors just sing out at you on a day like this."

"Sure do."

"Something special on your mind?"

"Sort of."

"Let me guess. . . . Eric's still not aware of you."

"Oh, Eric! What can I expect? He'd probably notice me all right if I couldn't double for a ruler."

"Looks shouldn't be any problem for you, Kim—not with those big, forget-me-not blue eyes and that lovely skin."

"Faces don't count. It's figures that matter. It's humiliating to be fifteen and still not have any excuse to buy a brassiere."

Ms. Davis laughed. "Anyway, looks aren't everything."

"No, but they matter a lot, don't they?"

"At your age, I suppose. It's too bad."

"Were you ever in love, Ms. Davis?"

"Lots of times." She didn't elaborate and I couldn't pry though I was curious. I guessed she was thirtyish and that not being pretty had had a lot to do with her not being married. Sure, plain-looking women wore wedding rings, but the man for Ms. Davis would have to be someone special, and special men probably didn't notice her.

"You know," Ms. Davis said hesitantly, "I don't know Eric all that well, but from what I've heard, you may be just as well off if he doesn't pay any attention to you."

"What have you heard?"

35

"Just rumors. He has an older brother who may not be the best influence on him. But I don't know for sure."

"Anyway, it doesn't matter," I said. "Eric's just a dream." I started edging toward the subject of the inheritance by asking, "Ms. Davis, if you had a lot of money, what would you do with it?"

Her eyes got a faraway look. "I'd accept an invitation I just got. Did you know the Greek boy who was an exchange student a couple of years back? No, you're a sophomore. He was before your time. Well, anyway, I correspond with him and—with certain members of his family. And they've invited me to be their guest in Athens for the summer. Can you imagine? Greece! The wine dark seas and all those ancient ruins! Just thinking about it gives me goose bumps."

"Couldn't you borrow the money? Fly now and pay later or something?"

"Only if I wanted bill collectors trailing me clear across the ocean," Ms. Davis said. "Only if I were really crazy instead of just mildly daft."

"Did you or did you not tell us Saroyan said everyone should be a little crazy some of the time?"

"I suspect he was talking about Armenians, not English teachers. English teachers had better not be crazy if they want to keep their jobs."

"Maybe you'll inherit a lot of money," I said.

"Maybe I will. Maybe one of Emma's schemes to make us rich will work after all." Ms. Davis laughed and went into a long description of what she called "Emma's hobby." Apparently, Emma occupied herself, when she wasn't baking, by entering contests and buying lottery tickets and answering chain letters—the kind where you send away five dollars and expect to win thousands. Ms. Davis acted half amused, half proud of her mother. "She's the financial genius in the family," Ms. Davis said.

"Is she good with money?" I asked.

"Better than I am anyway. I'm glad to hand my paycheck over to Emma and have her handle our finances. That way I don't worry, and she feels useful. It hurts her pride to be dependent on me. So Emma has her job and I have mine."

"But what about when it's a lot of money, like this Orlop thing?"

"What Orlop thing? Oh, you mean the possibility that we're in line to inherit millions? That's highly unlikely, Kim."

"But Emma thinks—"

"Emma has to have her dreams too."

"But if he's a con man . . . She gives him money, Ms. Davis!"

"She wouldn't invest much," Ms. Davis said. "Don't worry. She's a pretty shrewd lady."

"Did you know Orlop threatened me?" I asked, trying a different tack.

"Threatened you? About what?"

"He thinks I have some letter of his. He said I'd better give it to him or else."

"And you don't have it?"

"No."

"Well, I wouldn't take him too seriously," Ms. Davis said, patting my arm. "He strikes me as a weak, nervous person, a real mama's boy—which is probably why he's so enamored of Emma. Poor dear, she always did want a son to spoil. They're made for each other."

I gave up. Ms. Davis and I just weren't talking about the same man. No way. In fact, if I hadn't had Morey as witness, I would have begun to doubt my own impression of Malcolm Davis Orlop. Maybe I was foolish to be afraid of him. Maybe— but in the meantime, I was going to be very careful.

chapter five

The first thing I did when I got home was turn on all the lights. Next I checked the clock. Mother was due home at six. I started banging pots and clanging dishes energetically, getting dinner started to keep myself too busy to think.

It's amazing how safe you can feel inside your own home even if the windows are only glass and the doors aren't much less fragile. Our everything-within-reach efficiency kitchen has a ceiling full of lights that keep it bright as day and Mother has huge, spectacular pillows scattered all over the low white couch and chairs in the living room. Big, colorful paintings that are supposed to be dancing women cheer up the white walls even if the figures don't look much like women. The general mood of Mother's decorating is happy, or maybe just hopeful, but anyway I like it.

I was laying out forks and knives when, despite myself, I began thinking about Orlop. Was he going to be after me for the letter only at the Davises' house? He surely wouldn't hang around the high school and follow me home. Or would he?

I could get to school and back without going near the Davises by cutting across the fields behind the apartments. But suppose I met Orlop alone in an empty field? No, he wouldn't know about that shortcut—unless he knew my address, in which case, figuring out the shortest distance between here and the high school wouldn't be too hard. Not if he wanted to find me.

I looked down at my hands, wondering what those forks were doing in them. The brown rice that needs forty minutes to cook began boiling over on the stove. I got hold of myself and put the rice on to simmer. Then, to calm myself, I went to get my flute.

Sometimes when I'm feeling low I give a whole concert for the sole benefit of my good old kangaroo pal, Roo. Roo was taller than I was at age five when I first got him. Now he and his chair, a single bed, a four-drawer chest, and I just fit in my bedroom. Every Christmas Mother suggests I ought to give Roo to some toys-for-tots drive. Every Christmas I refuse. After all, who knows what kind of home he'd get. The truth is, I plan to take him off to college with me when I go. I'm loyal to old friends.

I played Roo a simple shepherd's tune for openers and was just getting into "Greensleeves" when Mother called my name. I dashed into the living room and hugged her as if I hadn't seen her in a week. "I'm so glad you're home," I said.

"Why? What's the matter?"

"Nothing. . . . Just . . . nothing."

Her face squeezed into the worry lines I hate most to cause. She always looks so worn down when she comes home, my mother. She tries too hard to get everything right—her job and raising me—and she ends up feeling inadequate. She says that's because *her* mother never thought she could do anything right. I think her mother is why Mother rarely criticizes me. Mostly she tells me what a fantastic daughter I am; she thinks praise is healthier than criticism. I must say I like her child-rearing methods.

"I smell something burning," I said. "Yipes, the rice!"

I rescued most of it and set the pot in the sink to soak while Mother started concocting one of her Chinese-style dishes with leftovers. She likes to eat. She's overweight and always in conflict between wanting to get rid of her bulges and wanting to eat. She says I'm lucky I take after my long, lean father. Personally, I think her big, blue eyes and good skin and curly hair are my luckiest inheritance.

"So how was your day?" I asked her.

"Bully. I figured out what's wrong between my boss and me."

"What's that?"

"He's under the impression that I'm not human.

To him, I'm a machine, one that pours out press releases in any required quantity on command. Would you believe that louse is sending me to Rochester tomorrow morning to interview some VIP he was told is a real stinker?"

"Oh no! Does that mean you won't be home for dinner tomorrow?"

"Won't be home at all, I'm afraid. I can't get a flight back until the next morning. Will you mind being alone very much, darling?"

"Yes. Yes, I do mind. Mother, can't you tell him to go himself?"

"I can, but—"

"Do you think he'll fire you?" I knew she thought her boss was just looking for an excuse to get rid of her so he could give her job to his girlfriend.

Mother hugged me. "Don't be silly," she said. I hugged her back, feeling comforted.

She went to call her boss. Our apartment is so small you can't avoid hearing phone conversations made in a normal tone of voice. She started out sounding strong, but he must have come on stronger because her pauses got longer and longer and then she began backing down. By the end of the conversation she was below ground level.

"Maybe you could check in with Jo Ann tomorrow and spend the night with her?" she said when she came back.

She sounded so pathetic that I reassured her,

"Mom, it's all right. That'll do fine. Don't feel bad."

I massaged the back of her neck, and she said some nice things about what a marvelous daughter I am. Also that she wished she had more guts. She was so tense. The muscles in the back of her neck always knot up when she's tense, and then she gets these headaches.

When Mother called, Jo Ann said sure, she'd be home tomorrow night, and I was welcome to bunk on her couch. That meant closing my eyes to the mess in her apartment and my nose to the stinky kitty litter pans she never seems to empty and the incense she's always burning to cover the smell. I hoped she wouldn't launch into one of her long monologues on the rottenness of the male sex besides.

After dinner I got a phone call. "Kim? This is Malcolm Orlop."

It was the bogyman himself. My hand gripped the receiver so hard I wouldn't have been surprised to hear it crack.

"Now don't hang up," he said. "I want to tell you about yesterday. I've been thinking why you did it, and I see how you were out to help Emma. She's a dear old lady, isn't she?"

I muttered agreement, wondering all the while how he had gotten my number. Unless Emma had let slip my last name. That was probably it.

"So you see," he said, "you don't have to worry

about protecting Emma from me. Like keeping that letter to hold over me. That's what you're doing, isn't it?"

"No," I said. "No."

"OK," he said. "We won't argue, but I want you to come over to the Davises' tomorrow. I'm going to show Emma some factual proof, some important documents that'll prove to you she's in line to inherit this money, she and her lovely daughter. Now will you trust me that far at least?"

"I don't know," I said. "I mean, I don't know if I can make it."

"Of course, you can make it. Don't disappoint me, Kim. I'm acting in good faith. I'm giving you the benefit of the doubt. You should do the same for me."

"But I don't have your letter."

"Uh-huh. I see."

"I really don't."

"You won't come?"

I hesitated, afraid to say I wouldn't. I could already hear the nasty tone creeping back into his voice. "I'll try to be there," I said, "but—"

"Good, good. That's a good girl. I'll see you tomorrow after school then at the Davises'. You'll see how wrong you are about me. I'm really quite a nice fellow." He chuckled as if to prove it.

When I hung up, Mother asked me to whom I'd been talking. "Just someone who wants to see me about something," I said. "It's nothing important."

"You seem distressed, Kim. What's wrong, darling?"

"Nothing, Mother. Just a mood. You know how I am." I smiled for her.

It was only in bed that night while I listened to the dull thuds in the air ducts and tried to get to sleep that I realized something. Now Orlop had my telephone number. He could reach me anytime he wanted. At midnight I was still twisting around, trying to find a good position to fall asleep in.

In the morning Mother came into the living room all dressed up in her good, gray suit with the real gold chain that my father had given her on their tenth anniversary just before he told her he was leaving her. She looked elegant, and I told her so, even though her suitcase had a broken latch, and the rope tied around it sort of botched the picture.

"Maybe I ought to let him fire me," she said. "I never seem to get time to spend with you anymore, baby. You're going to grow up behind my back, and then you'll be too old to need me around."

"Mom, don't be dumb. Didn't we have a great time camping together this summer?"

"We did, didn't we?" She smiled. "For two non-campers, we did well. And it was fun, wasn't it?"

"Mom, I think you're a wonderful mother. Stop worrying."

My noble behavior was rewarded that day. I got to school, late as usual, but Morey is my lab partner, and he always covers for me. Mr. Kramer, our bio teacher, never gives the girls a hard time anyway. But it's what happened after biology that was my reward. I was speeding down the hall toward the music room, which is down in the basement at the other end of the building, when who should call my name but—right! Eric of the Genghis Khan eyes. "Kim," he said, and my heart cartwheeled out of my chest, leaving me standing dead in my tracks gawking up at him.

"Wanna go to the game with me Friday night?" he asked.

"This Friday night?"

"Yeah."

"Sure." I didn't know what game he was talking about, but who cared so long as Eric—tall, beautiful Eric—wanted to take me someplace.

"I could pick you up. My brother's driving."

"OK," I said. "I live in the Van Worth Apartments. Ours is the third one in on your right."

"Yeah," he said and walked off. I watched his fair hair gleaming high above the crowd until he disappeared into a room. When I remembered to start breathing again, I continued on my way to music.

Mr. C. glared at me for being three minutes late and told me to report to the detention room after school, but that didn't affect me at all, not until he said, "Now wipe that silly grin off your face and get to work." He tapped the back of a chair with his baton for the group's attention.

46

Mr. C. doesn't put up with nonsense from anyone, but it's probably due to him our high school orchestra is so good. I went meekly to my place only to realize with horror that I didn't have my flute. Then I practically sank into the floor with embarrassment.

"Pretend," Mr. C. snarled when he saw my predicament. "Pretend!"

So I stood there for forty minutes blowing an imaginary flute and feeling like a fool.

chapter six

Detention was beautiful—forty five minutes with nothing to do but daydream about Eric and no need to feel guilty because I should be doing my math homework or some other chore. In detention you're just supposed to sit. Only afterward, when I was cutting across the field going home, did I remember Orlop. Five o'clock, and that colorless sky above me would soon disappear into darkness.

Ahead of me browned, knee-high weeds stretched away to a dark frame of trees where I thought I saw a figure moving. I stopped on the dirt path, ignoring the grasses tickling my bare legs, and considered. To get to the apartments, I had to pass between the black trees and through the narrow opening in the chain link fence, then down the short slope into the development. Nothing was moving now. Probably it had been my imagination. Or it might have been somebody walking his dog.

When I got near the trees, I sprinted through the opening in the fence, leaping down the slippery flagstones lining the slope and ending up at my apartment door out of breath. There I stopped to think. I'd promised Orlop I'd meet him at the Davises. It was late, but if I didn't go over and apologize for not showing up, he'd think I'd lied and get mad at me again. If I went now, though, I'd have to come home alone in the dark. That wasn't too promising. The best thing to do was to call and explain why I couldn't make it. Yes, that was the way to go.

I fumbled for my keys while I scanned the parking lot. Some cars were already parked nose up to our two-story apartment buildings, which cluster around a central lawn and swimming pool. The cars and lighted kitchen windows meant people were home from work and busy preparing dinners. Now if Jo Ann were home, too, I'd be fine. Maybe I wouldn't even move in with her for the night. I could just sort of check in.

Jo Ann's bedroom is next to our front door. I noticed that her windows were dark when I unlocked the door, but she could be in her kitchen, which was under ours. Our balcony overhung her terrace. I ran upstairs, switched lights on all over the apartment, bent over the wrought iron railing on our balcony and saw the lights in Jo Ann's kitchen. Good.

Next I called the Davises. "Oh, Malcolm's already left, Kim," Emma told me. "He was upset you didn't come."

"Emma, did you tell him I didn't have his letter?"

"Well, I told him I couldn't imagine why you'd want to keep anything that was his. I said as far as I know you're an honest girl. Anyway, Morey told him you didn't have the letter."

"Morey was there?"

"Yes. He kept bothering poor Malcolm with questions. I know Malcolm was annoyed with him. I don't know what gets into Morey sometimes, and you know what Malcolm showed me, Kim? A photograph of a headstone that was my late husband's Uncle Charles', and a copy of a birth certificate that proves that Uncle Charles was the nephew of that Percy Lambreth Davis who left all the billions behind. So we are bona fide heirs."

"Really, Emma? That's wonderful."

"Yes, I'm pleased."

"When will you get the money?"

Emma explained at great length that all the registered heirs as a group would have to fight the claim in court. It would take time, but Malcolm knew a lawyer who had an in with the judges and might get them an early hearing. "We could have it all settled and be getting our share in just a few months," Emma said enthusiastically.

"That would be terrific."

"Yes. Deirdre is still pooh-poohing the whole

thing, but she'll change her tune when I put the check in her hand."

"Do you think Mr. Orlop was mad at me for not showing up, Emma?"

"No. Why should he be mad at you? Morey said you had to stay after school because you got to class late or something."

"That's right." I wondered how Morey had known, or had he just lied for me?

After I finished talking to Emma, I called Jo Ann and said I'd do some homework and maybe not even come down to sleep at all. Everything seemed to be normal and I felt safe enough. Jo Ann sounded relieved. She told me she was coming down with a dilly of a cold and planned to take an antihistamine and go right to bed. I sympathized and said to let me know if she needed anything. When you live alone and get sick, taking care of yourself is depressing, also difficult.

I snacked on leftovers cold from the refrigerator and was washing out my prettiest sweater to wear for Friday night when Morey called.

"Private investigator Stern here. Is this my partner to whom I am speaking, maybe?" he joked.

"Maybe it is I, Stern. How's every little thing by you?"

"Can't complain. Although my little sister got paint all over the lab notes that have to be turned in Friday."

"Our lab notes have to be in Friday?"

"Sure. Didn't you hear Kramer? He made a big deal of it."

I groaned. "That's what I get for coming in late."

"You weren't late. I distinctly remember you sitting there with your gorgeous blue eyes fixed right on Kramer."

"I don't remember a thing."

"Probably you were thinking about your hoop hero."

"Hoop hero?"

"Right, hoop hero. You know, Eric, the overgrown weed who plays basketball."

"What makes you think I'd be thinking about Eric?" I was horrified. Did it show that obviously? Was the whole school laughing at me for being gone on him?

"Now, now, don't panic," said Morey the mind reader. "I just happened to notice the way you were looking at him one day."

I grunted, as embarrassed as if I'd been caught in the boys' locker room.

"Hey," Morey said. "What's the big deal? So you like Eric. Probably nobody else has even noticed. After all, how many people know you well enough to read what's in your eyes?"

"That sounds sexy."

"Yeah," he said with a funny downhill slope in his voice that puzzled me and made me wonder exactly how Morey felt about me.

"Anyway," he said. "Don't you want to know what I've discovered?"

"Sure. I hear you were my stand-in at the Davises today."

"Right. Your old pal Orlop got his stomach full of me and my nosy questions."

"So what did you learn?"

Morey was almost as long-winded as Emma. He went into detail about how Orlop had shown them a dozen different documents, a whole smorgasbord of copies of court records that he only allowed them ten seconds to study. Orlop also had lists of securities and land holdings that Percy Lambreth Davis had once held, even a copy of a probate court's decree indicating Percy Lambreth Davis's money should be distributed to his rightful heirs. A wife had already inherited half the money. It sounded impressive to me. "Morey, enough!" I said finally. "Do you think there's money in it for Emma or not?"

"I don't know. It's possible. But I caught a glimpse of a check Emma handed him for three hundred and fifty bucks. That's supposed to cover his expenses while he does research to establish her claim—like make a family tree. And he has to send to Texas for records to prove her husband's Uncle Charlie was born there, or some rigamarole like that. The thing that really worries me is Orlop's already hinting about bigger expenses. Ms. Davis may never retrieve her trusty heap from Elwood's."

"What expenses?"

"Oh, lawyer's fees so they can pursue the case. They might have to pay off certain individuals in some big bank. Orlop claims the assets of the estate are deliberately being concealed from the rightful heirs."

"Where would Emma get more money if she can't even pay their bills?"

"Borrow against the house. It's in her name."

"Oh, no!"

"Orlop says she's got to be willing to invest money if she expects to make any, and Emma agrees."

"But suppose it's a fraud?"

"Sickening to contemplate, isn't it?"

I suggested we go back to the police, but Morey pointed out we had no more concrete evidence to show them than we'd had before. There wasn't even a receipt for the money Emma had given Orlop today. He had told her the cancelled check would be her receipt. He left nothing in her hands. All papers went back into his attaché case. Even his business cards lacked an address or phone number that could be traced.

"Besides," Morey said, "Emma's so convinced he's going to bring her a fortune that she'd never bring charges against him on just our suspicions."

"What can we do then?" I asked, feeling frustrated.

"Don't know. Wait for Emma to change her

mind? I tried riling up Ms. Davis, but she just smiled and told me about the way Emma comes out a winner in bingo games. I get the idea being in charge of their finances is supposed to be mental health medicine for Emma."

"You got it," I said. "Do you think Orlop will disappear with their money if he's a crook?"

"Maybe, or it could be he'll come back for more."

I shook my head. It made me angry to leave Orlop a clear field to go on cheating the Davises.

"Listen, the main thing is that he hasn't bothered you again," Morey said. "He hasn't, has he?"

"I haven't seen him."

"Good. He's probably decided you really don't have his letter. . . . Now, about the lab notebook. You want me to help you with it?"

Morey was such a good kid. I was tempted, but I'd never copied anybody else's work, and I didn't want to start now. "No, thanks," I said. "I'll see what I can do with what I've got."

After we hung up, I spent about an hour on the mess of lab notations and got so frustrated at some of the stuff I just couldn't figure out, much less put in the format Mr. Kramer wanted to see it in, that I gave up. I'd work on them over the weekend and hand them in late.

It was awfully quiet in the apartment. I had to keep reminding myself that all the creaking footsteps were just noises from the heating ducts. The refrigerator hummed along with the breathy sound of the hot air rising in the ducts, and the feeling that something was in the apartment with me was just a feeling. I flicked on the television to keep me company, but nothing was on but cops and robbers and a comedy that was too stupid to be funny. The music on the FM station was Wagner, which I don't particularly like. Finally I took my flute, filled the tub and put in some of the bubble bath Mother had given me for my birthday. I took off my clothes in the bedroom and carried my cozy fleece robe with me to the bathroom. I'm sure I didn't close the bedroom door behind me. Why should I have? I did close the bathroom door, though, to keep the steam in. I was in the bathtub for maybe an hour, tootling away in the warm, silky water and making up my own music.

When I came out of the bathroom, I noticed two things. The door to my bedroom was closed, and a draft was coming from the sliding glass door to the balcony . . . which was open. It was as if a long needle had jabbed me. One jolt sent me from calm to hysterical. In two seconds flat I was out the door, down the stairs, around the building and banging on Jo Ann's door, shivering in my bathrobe from the chilly air and terror. No answer. Her car was there, butted up to the building, but no lights were on. I couldn't understand it until I remembered her cold and the antihistamine. An antihistamine tablet had knocked me into oblivion once, too.

I caromed across the grass courtyard to the Spencers. They're an elderly couple who have a poodle I play with sometimes. At least they knew me to say hello to. The Spencers let me in, all agog over my running around in mid-October in nothing but a bathrobe and bare feet.

"Can I use your phone?"

"Of course, of course." Mrs. Spencer started making hot cocoa for me while I called the police.

"Sergeant Morton," the voice answered.

"Sergeant Morton!" I cried, so happy it was someone I knew. "This is Kim Terrell. You know, the girl who came to see you about that man who grabbed my arm and the inheritance that the Davises—"

"Yes, what's the trouble?" he interrupted me.

"I think someone came into my apartment." I heard the Spencers gasping behind me. I explained about the doors, and Sergeant Morton said to stay right where I was. Ten minutes later I was drinking my hot cocoa and petting Pierre, the poodle, when Mr. Spencer, who had gone out to see what was happening, bustled back in.

"You ought to see them. They're like flies, those police cars. Coming in from everywhere. Must have sent out a call to the city for help. Some of them went up to your apartment, Kim. Should be interesting if they catch him in the act, huh?"

Mr. Spencer looked as if he were enjoying the

whole thing. Mrs. Spencer told him he was awful, but that didn't dampen his enthusiasm at all. I think he was terribly disappointed when Sergeant Morton came to the door and told me, "Well, we checked your apartment, but there's no sign of anyone. No sign anybody's been there at all, in fact. Did you happen to go out on the balcony when you came home today?"

"Oh, well, yes, I did."

"I see. . . . You know, it's possible you left that door open by mistake."

"What about my bedroom door being closed?"

"Well, you could have closed that behind you without thinking. You know, we do lots of things unconsciously." He was gently telling me I'd sent out a false alarm.

"But I always close and lock the sliding doors behind me, always."

"Yeah, well, anyway you ought to keep a stick in the track. That would keep any intruders out. Without a stick, those doors are real easy to open. You ought to get a stick just as a normal safety precaution."

"Yes," I said. "I'll tell my mother."

"Mother gone again tonight?" He sounded sympathetic but over the wrong thing.

"Yes."

He nodded his head for a few seconds then asked, "And your dad, where's he?"

"He lives in California."

He nodded again. "So you live all alone with your mother?"

This time I nodded. I'd told him that at the station.

"Maybe you ought to sleep over at a friend's house when your mother has to stay out late. That possible?"

I got the message. He thought I'd just scared myself and there hadn't been anybody in my apartment at all. "OK, I'll do that."

"But just to be sure," he said, "we'll send somebody over to dust for fingerprints in the morning. We'll have to take your fingerprints and your mother's and those of anybody else who's been in the apartment recently. Any problem there?"

"My mother doesn't know about Orlop."

"Why not?"

"I didn't want her to have something else to worry about."

He shook his head. "Not smart. Not smart at all. You'd better tell her. We'll come by early. Be sure you don't touch the sliding door or the frame around it or the bedroom door."

"OK, thanks," I said. "I'm sorry I bothered you."

"That's what we're here for." The sergeant waved good-bye and left.

I was embarrassed. The Spencers wanted to keep me in their apartment, but I called Jo Ann. The phone is right next to her bed, so this time she did wake up. She said to come right on over. I collected my clothes and my own blanket and pillow and stretched out on her couch with one of her cats curled up inside the crook of my leg. I was so exhausted that I fell asleep in spite of the smell of the cat pans.

chapter seven

The policeman who came to dust for fingerprints Wednesday morning was a talkative, gray-haired man with a lumpy nose. As he worked, he explained to me how you transfer the image of the prints to film and study the prints for certain points.

It takes at least nine points to distinguish an individual's prints, and you need prints from more than one finger. Next you compare prints to make sure the ones you've identified don't belong to any people living in or visiting the house legitimately. If you do come up with identifiable prints that can't be accounted for, you send them over to the Department of Criminal Justice System, the D.C.J.S., in Albany, where the experts run the card through a computer to see if the person has ever been arrested. It was interesting. I was sorry Morey wasn't there to hear the whole thing.

Anyway, while the policeman was working and

explaining it all to me, Mother walked in, suitcase in hand. "Kim, what happened? Are you all right?" she cried.

"I'm all right. Nothing's happened. I'm all right," I said, but the wild look didn't leave her eyes, and I knew telling her the whole story, which I was about to do, wasn't going to calm her down any.

First, I explained that the policeman was just dusting for fingerprints, but that they didn't really think anyone had broken in. Then, I made her put her suitcase down and told her slowly, in great detail, about Orlop and me and the letter and the inheritance scheme—if it was a scheme. Mother reacted a lot less emotionally than I'd expected, but she agreed that Orlop sounded like a crook. She didn't understand why the police couldn't do something about it.

When we went down to the police station and had our prints taken, Mother made Sergeant Morton explain all over again how the best way to work up a fraud case was to get evidence the swindler was using the mail, which allowed the U.S. Postal Inspection Service to become involved.

"See, then it's a federal case and you got something worth prosecuting," Sergeant Morton said. At Mother's urging, he did promise to try to find out if Orlop had any kind of criminal record.

Afterward, Mother decided we both needed a treat, so she took me for breakfast at the pancake house. I had blueberry waffles with whipped cream as my antidote to the whole business. Mother had an English muffin.

"You must have been scared out of your wits," Mother said. "I should never have gone on that trip and left you all alone. I don't know why you didn't go down to Jo Ann's right away, though."

"Bad judgment," I said.

I watched her sneak a forkful of my waffle and dunk it in the whip cream. Orlop seemed comfortably remote at that moment.

"What I'll do is tell Connie I can't make her party this Friday night," Mother was saying. "I'm not leaving you alone nights for a while."

"That's silly, Mom. Also unnecessary. Friday night I've got a date."

"With whom?"

"Eric."

"Eric, your dream man?"

"That's the one."

"Lovely, darling! Tell me all about it. How did he ask you? Where's he taking you?" Mother was a lot more at ease with boys as the subject than with fraud and criminals and people breaking into our apartment.

"He asked me out of the blue, just stopped me in the hall and asked. I didn't even know he knew my name. And he's taking me to a game."

"What kind of a game?"

"He didn't say. Probably something to do with a ball, basketball maybe. His brother's driving."

"Umm. What are you going to wear?"

"The sweater that matches my eyes with the frill around the neck."

She laughed. "Be careful. You don't want to turn him on too far."

"Mom, you forget. The sweater can only do so much when there's nothing but me under it."

Mother promptly launched into a lecture about the importance of liking your own body and how breasts are overemphasized in our society and are a sexist hang-up that women should not let men foist on them. Since my father left her, Mother's become very sensitive to feminine issues.

She wound up with her usual, "It isn't what you have, but how you feel about yourself that makes you beautiful." That's her theme song. I think she's trying to convince herself as much as me. She's the one who is always going on diets. As for me, I see my defects all right, but I like myself pretty well— or parts of me. Anyway, it was a lovely breakfast, and I avoided thinking about Orlop until I got to school.

I was about to enter Mr. Kramer's class on time for a change. Since he never reacted to my being late, I was eager to see his reaction to my being on time. However, I backed away from the door obediently when Morey called, "Kim, come over here. I've got to talk to you."

I joined Morey in the dead airspace in the corner

of the stairwell. Kids spiraled up past us in a hurry to get to classes.

"Urgent business," Morey said.

"Such as?"

"This morning my alarm clock went berserk and woke me at six, so I decided to make use of my extra hours of wakefulness and go rake some leaves for the Davises. Guess what I found?"

"A magic mushroom."

"Not that good."

"A winning sweepstakes ticket."

"Come on. The bell's going to ring."

"So what did you find?"

"The evidence!"

"Orlop?"

"A letter that Orlop wrote asking some guy to bring money someplace. Trouble is, it's not too legible from a week of sitting under a pile of wet leaves."

"You think that's the letter he thought I took?"

"Bet you it is."

"But why should he care about a letter he wrote himself? Unless you think it might have spelled out his whole plan or something."

"No, no. See, he *mailed* that letter and it was returned to him stamped wrong address. Now the point is, once you use the U.S. mail to defraud someone, you're asking for big trouble because the U.S. Postal Inspectors can get you sent up for years."

"I know. I know. I heard Sergeant Morton's lecture too, remember?" The bell had rung and the halls were empty. One late student took the stairs three at a time and bolted past us.

"Orlop hasn't bothered you since the phone call, has he?"

I thought of the closed bedroom door and the open sliding door, but that had been my own nervousness. At least, Sergeant Morton thought it was. "Maybe you convinced him I don't have his letter," I said.

"Well, we do have it now, but let's not let him know that."

"Yeah," I said. "Let's give the police the evidence and hope they can get Emma's money back."

"Right, but first I'm going to get my father to make some copies for me."

When Morey and I finally sneaked into biology lab, late as usual, Mr. Kramer didn't even look up.

chapter eight

Getting a personal phone call in our high school is a rare event. It only happens for some terrible disaster like a death in the family or a forgotten dentist's appointment. When the secretary's voice coming through the intercom said I was wanted in the office for a phone call, I stood up in bewilderment. A kid who knows me from orchestra whispered, "Forget your flute again?"

I shook my head and hesitated over whether to take my books or leave them. It was close to the end of the last period of the day, and the school buses were already lined up outside awaiting our mass exit. Our social studies teacher raised her voice irritably calling the class to attention so she could finish what she'd been saying about Vercingetorix. I picked up my books and purse and swung out of the room, avoiding her glare.

Who could be calling me? It could only be Mother. Another trip? Not this soon after the last one. If it was another trip, I was going to protest.

Mother was getting too good at letting herself be used, and I couldn't take much more of being alone, expecting Orlop to step out of every dark shadow. Or maybe something bad had happened—an accident? By the time I'd run out of worry ideas, I was at the office. Old Sourface, the secretary, who had permanent tracks between her eyebrows, pointed at the phone that showed a lit button. It was sitting on an empty desk right out in the open.

"Don't keep the line busy too long. It's almost 3:30 you know."

I had the urge to tell her it wasn't my fault someone had called me, but I kept my mouth shut and meekly picked up the receiver instead. "Hi?"

"Kim Terrell?" a crackling male voice asked.

"Yes."

"This is the police calling. We've got a few questions for you concerning the letter."

"What letter?"

"You know, the letter that belongs to Mr. Malcolm Orlop, the one you delivered to us, that letter."

"I didn't deliver any letter to you."

"You didn't?"

"No, there must be some mistake."

"I see. You're sure of that now?"

"I'm sure," I said. "If—in fact, how come you know about the letter? I mean, where did you hear—?"

"Never mind that. We've got our ways of getting information. Now, listen, you can just forget this. So long as you didn't deliver it to the police like you say, it's OK. Just forget the whole thing."

The crackling voice had been going faster and faster. Suddenly there was a gasp, and from far away I heard the sound of breaking glass and a choked cry and what sounded like music. The music came up loud over everything. Music in a police station?

I said, "Hey, who are you?" Then the phone went dead.

I put the receiver back on the hook, looked away from the secretary's disapproving eyes, and walked out to the hall. My knees went limp. I had to lean against the speckled composition wall to keep from falling. Even school wasn't safe. He could reach me anywhere. What could I do? I had no doubt Orlop was behind that phone call. He'd found an ac-complice—in a bar maybe—told him he wanted to play a joke on someone, or paid him to make the phone call.

Orlop always had been sure I had the letter even before Morey found it. Now he was trying to find out if I'd given his letter to the police yet. I should have said I didn't have the letter. Had I made that clear? Morey had the letter. I didn't have it. What had I said? I couldn't remember exactly. I tried to rerun the conversation in my head, but I couldn't concentrate. All I wanted to do really was sit down and cry. I wanted my mother to be there. I wanted her to put her arms around me and pat me on the back and say everything would be OK.

The bell rang. In seconds, ant streams of homeward-bound kids filled the halls, pushing and running over each other in their impatience to get outside the doors into the freedom of their afternoons. I didn't move. I couldn't risk walking home. Nor did I want to be in the apartment alone. I thought of taking the school bus. I never took it because it circled around town for an hour and a half before it got to my apartment project, but at least I would be safe on it, although even an hour and a half on the bus would still leave a gap of an hour before Mother got home from work. Alone in that apartment, I'd be a sitting duck for Orlop.

I waited until the stampede was over. Then I went to the pay phone near the front door. I didn't have the right change, so I had to race back to the office where I caught Old Sourface covering her typewriter and locking her desk way before time. I guessed the principal was out for the day.

When I asked her if I could use the school phone, she said no, as I expected. Then I asked her for change, and she slammed around in a drawer where she kept the petty cash to let me know I was inconveniencing her. I thanked her anyway when she handed me my change. Maybe she had a horrible home life. Back at the pay phone, I dialed, praying

Mother would be at her desk. To my relief, she answered immediately.

"Mom, I'm at school. Could you come and get me?"

"Why, Kim? What's wrong?"

"I just got this phone call, in *school,* Mom. It was from Orlop. I know it was."

"What did he want?"

"He wanted to know if I'd given that letter to the police yet."

"What letter? Kim, you told me you don't have the letter."

"Morey found it. He has it."

"So?"

"So, Mom, now Orlop is sure I have it. He's going to come after me."

"Oh, no! Are you sure? You say he called you in school? I can't imagine the school would put through a call to a student from just anybody."

"Well, they did. He had somebody else call me and say they were the police."

"The police? It wasn't your Mr. Orlop's voice? And the person said he was a policeman? Then what makes you so sure he wasn't?"

"Because the police couldn't have known about the letter since— Oh, Mom, just believe me. It was Orlop, and I want you to come pick me up so I don't have to go home alone!"

"Darling, calm down. You can't be sure what the

police know and what they don't know. Maybe you're imagining things. Remember last night when you called the police because you thought he'd been in our apartment? I'll tell you what we'll do. You call the police station and ask if anyone there did call you at school. If they say no, call me right back and I'll come and get you. OK?"

"I know it was Orlop."

"Sweetheart, it'll only take you a minute to call. And whatever they say, call me back so I'll know."

"All right." I put the receiver back on the hook, wishing Mother had been more emotional and less logical and were on her way to rescue me. She thought I was hysterical. That hurt. It was bad enough to be scared without being misjudged besides. Automatically, I lifted the phone book hanging from a chain on the side of the post and looked up the number of the police station. I dialed and asked to speak to Officer Morton.

"He's not in this afternoon. Can I help you? I'm Sergeant Papandopolus."

"I need to find out if anyone at the station just called the high school and asked to speak to Kim Terrell."

"Who are you?"

"Kim Terrell."

"Somebody playing a trick on you?" He sounded sympathetic. "Wait a second, and I'll check. Hang on."

I waited. Outside the big plate glass window,

around the circle that was now empty of school buses, was a clump of half-grown spruces. I saw a profile, a man's head with a receding hairline; someone was standing behind a tree out there, someone who could be Orlop. I squeezed tight with terror. The only other open exit from the building was through the library at the side. From where the man was standing, he could see both the front and side exits. And he was waiting—for me.

"What?" I asked the voice now back on the line and saying something to me.

"I said nobody from this station called the high school today for anyone," Sergeant Papandopolus said. "So you can be sure it was a prank call, sis."

"Thank you," I said. I hung up and hurried to get out of sight of the window, scurrying down the hall toward Ms. Davis's room. The hall was depressingly empty. Ms. Davis's door was locked. I tried the faculty room, even daring to stick my head in and ask the two teachers having coffee there if they knew where Ms. Davis was.

They said they had no idea and turned away, but one offered over his shoulder, "She's probably at some meeting."

"Probably," the other agreed.

I whispered a thanks and backed out of their inner sanctum. The halls looked even emptier. I could hear my own footsteps. There was no help anywhere. I thought of hiding in the girls' room until six o'clock, but I wasn't that desperate. I remembered that I hadn't called Mother back, turned and started toward the phone. I stopped short when I thought of how exposed that pay phone was, suspended from two poles in front of the plate glass window. He would see me plainly from his hiding place in the clump of spruce. I reversed my direction again and set off for the library, which might still be open. The head custodian came around the corner toward me, carrying a ladder and an electric drill.

"Hi, Mr. Milton. Could you help me, please?"

"Depends," he said. "What's the problem? Locker stuck?"

"Nothing like that. There's a man outside. I think he's trying to follow me, and I'm scared to go home. Could you just see if he's still out there?"

"A man? What's he following you for?"

"It's a long story. Could you just check for me, please?"

"What's he look like?"

"Just ordinary, kind of colorless, not much hair left, blue eyes."

He looked hard at me to see if I was playing a joke on him, then said, "OK, I'll look." He leaned his ladder against the wall and set off for the front entrance.

I squatted on the floor against the wall, so tired I would have been happy to just stay put there. A clock bulged out from the wall a little way down the hall. Almost four o'clock. Still two hours until

Mother got home. Where could I go? Morey was at an all day meeting in New York City for high school magazine editors and advisors. I thought of calling up one of the girls I eat lunch with and inviting myself over to her house, but none of them lived anywhere near the school. Mother was still waiting for me to call her back. I wished Mr. Milton would hurry.

I was still staring at the clock when it hit me. How could Orlop have finished his phony phone call and gotten to the high school so fast? I'd heard music in the background. . . . There was no bar near here, but the call could have come from some-body's home. The small, respectable houses in the neighborhood surrounding the school seemed un-likely, though. He wasn't going to be able to talk any of those lawn-tending, tax-paying citizens into making a fake call to the high school for him. So where had he called from?

"There's nobody out there now," Mr. Milton told me, picking up his ladder. "I went outside and took a good look around."

"Thank you very much," I said, grateful that somebody at least was willing to help me out. The shape I'd seen might have been some boy waiting for someone. Orlop was probably miles away. Doing what? Figuring out a way to get back his precious letter. No way was I going back to the apartment alone.

The phone was safe now. I decided to call Mother

back and trudged down the hall. There was no one outside that I could see as I put my books down and searched in my change purse for money. No change. Mother must be plenty worried about me by now. I traced Mr. Milton, by the whine of his drill, to a room near the library.

"You wouldn't have any change on you, would you Mr. Milton? I have to make a phone call."

He felt around in his pockets and shook his head. "All's I got is a nickle and some pennies if that'll do you any good."

"No, thanks." I took a deep breath and walked out the library exit from the school, sick of its echoing emptiness anyway. The huge parking lot held only a stranded bus and a handful of cars. The few leaves left on the trees were dry, dead, rattly ones. The sky was already dimming out for evening; at six it would be dark out. I hesitated, trying to think of where to go, then started walking toward the front of the school.

A public bus that follows the main road past the high school to the mall came into view. Its brightly lit interior looked like a haven to me. With a surge of energy, I ran to the road and then, unsure where the bus stop was, along the side of the road, waving at the bus to get the driver to stop. He passed me without a glance and stopped at a corner so far ahead I knew I'd never be able to make it before he started off again.

An old lady clambered off, taking her time. The

bus doors folded shut, but just then the light turned red, so the driver had to wait after all. I banged on the door just as the light turned green again. For a second I thought the driver was going to ignore me, but then he opened the doors to let me in. I was breathing so hard, I couldn't talk. I handed him a dollar and got change enough to make the phone call to Mother as soon as I got off at the mall.

"Where were you?" she demanded. "I was frantic when you didn't call back. Are you all right?"

"I'm at the mall. Can you pick me up in front of the Boston Store on your way home from work?"

"Sure, fine. Are you all right?"

"More or less. The police said they didn't call me. It was Orlop, Mother."

"Or some kid being funny."

"Nobody knows about the letter except Morey, and he wouldn't do that to me. Besides, he's in New York for the day."

"Kim, I don't know. If all this is really happening, we should do something to protect you, but I don't know what."

"See you at six," I said.

"Darling? You're not mad at me because I doubted your suspicions, are you?"

"It's all right, Mother. I know it seems hard to believe. You're used to dealing with regular people, and Orlop's a criminal."

"All right. We'll talk about it at dinner. Will you be OK?"

"Sure," I said and hung up. I was a little angry with her, but at least the mall felt safe to me—all those open store fronts and people with shopping to do. I meandered around and finally settled down on a bench in front of the merry-go-round. A little kid of three or four was the only one on the machine. He was going round and round with both hands gripping the pole of his horse, and he looked too scared to be enjoying himself. I knew just how he felt.

chapter nine

Mother had had plenty of time to think over her reaction to my call for help by the time she picked me up. As usual when considering her own behavior, she decided she'd done wrong. Nobody eats up guilt the way my mother does. She licks it up like excess calories. At dinner she apologized four times for letting me down.

"After all, even if I had been right about the phone call being legitimate—which I wasn't—I should have dropped everything and come. I promise, Kim, I'll never let you down again. Do you forgive me?"

"Mother, nothing happened. So as it turned out, you were right. I didn't even see Orlop. I guess he just wanted to find out where the letter was, and your idea about calling the police was just good sense. You didn't let me down." I didn't tell her about the man in the bushes. That had probably been my imagination anyway.

"But—all right," Mother said. "I did say I'd come

when you called back, didn't I? And I meant it."

"And it wasn't your fault I didn't have change for the phone."

She smiled at me. "How about if I drive you to school again tomorrow morning?"

"Great."

The next morning Mother was in good spirits even though driving me meant quite a detour for her. She was high on the prospect of her boss getting promoted out of their office, thereby improving the quality of Mother's life.

"Now, I'm not going to count on it too much," she kept saying. "Besides, who knows, I might be saddled with an even worse boss."

"Or you might get his job yourself."

"No chance of that. He hasn't given me a decent job evaluation ever. I'm just lucky he hasn't gotten me fired."

"Think positively," I said. "You're a bright, talented, hard-working publicity person. You're the best."

"I am?" She smiled as I started frowning at her. I was going to yell if she began putting herself down now. "Of course I am," she said. "Kim?"

"What?"

"You're not still scared, are you?"

"I'm OK," I said. "Tomorrow night's my date with Eric. I'm going to think about that."

"Good, and remember, if you need me—"

"I'll call."

She wouldn't let me out of the car before she'd given me a hug and a kiss, a little embarrassing since we were smack in front of the school. "I'm lucky to have a daughter like you," Mother said.

"Don't get schmaltzy," I said, borrowing one of Morey's words for something that was too sentimental.

Mother drove off smiling. I left my jacket in my locker and picked up the copy of Carson McCullers' *The Heart Is a Lonely Hunter* that Ms. Davis had lent me. I'd meant to return it to her yesterday. I wanted to tell her what a great book it was, one of the best I've ever read.

Ms. Davis usually got in early, and unlike most of the other teachers, she didn't spend much time socializing in the faculty room. She would probably be in her room organizing what she needed for her teaching that day. I ambled down the hall to her room, thinking about my blue sweater and whether I'd get a chance to ask Eric how come he had suddenly decided to ask me for a date. I had wondered about it and couldn't come up with a good answer. If our evening went as well as I hoped, I'd ask him.

Ms. Davis was on her hands and knees digging books out of the back of a cupboard. "Hi, can I help?" I asked.

She looked over her shoulder. "Kim! You know, I was just having a conversation with you in my head."

"About what?"

"About our mutual friend, Malcolm Orlop."

"He's no friend of mine," I said and sat down at a desk near her, sobered by the mere sound of his name. "What's he been up to at your house lately?"

"Are you in a bad mood?" she asked, looking at me carefully.

"No, I was in a good one, but—did you know I got called to the phone in school yesterday?"

"No."

"And guess who got somebody to pretend to be a police officer to ask me about the letter I'd sent to the police—which, of course, I hadn't sent since I don't have it."

"Kim, really! Why would Malcolm want to do that?"

"To find out if the police have the letter yet. Honestly, Ms. Davis, it's true. I checked with the police station, and they said no one there called me."

"Maybe the call was made from some other police station."

"How would any other one know my name?"

"I don't know. But the idea of Malcolm going to such lengths over some letter seems farfetched."

"Well, we'll see. Morey found the letter, and he *is* going to give it to the police."

"So you *do* have Orlop's letter!"

"Well, I didn't before, but we do now. Anyway, it's no big deal. It's in such bad condition that all you can see is the postmark and a few words. It won't prove much one way or the other."

I explained about the U.S. Postal Inspectors making a federal case out of any attempt to defraud people by use of the mails, and told Ms. Davis that mail fraud means years in prison instead of just a fine or a few days in jail.

"All I can say is, I hope you're wrong," she said uneasily. "Emma's given Malcolm a lot of money, but—I'm sure his intentions are honorable. He's not a very clever man, but I'm certain he's harmless. For instance, do you know why he became a genealogist?" She began stacking the books on the counter as she talked.

"No, and I don't really care," I said. It shook me that Ms. Davis wouldn't be convinced. I could understand my mother's not believing Orlop was rotten. *She* had never met him, but Ms. Davis ought to be a better judge of character.

"Kim, surely your mind's not closed to understanding the man?" Ms. Davis said.

I sighed. Being open-minded is a chore sometimes. "Go ahead. Tell me about him."

"Apparently his interest in genealogy came from listening to his mother. She was as fascinated by the relationships of all the families in their town as some people are by soap operas. From what Malcolm says, he and his mother were inseparable until she died two years ago. He's still lonely for her. Now isn't that pathetic, for a grown man to be such a mama's boy?"

"He could be a pathetic swindler, couldn't he?"

Ms. Davis's features knotted into thought. "No," she said finally. "At least, not where Emma is concerned. He loves Emma. I'm sure he does. She feeds him and fusses over him the way his mother used to. I can't believe he would cheat her. His eyes melt when he looks at her, and you should hear them chattering away together. I'm sure he sincerely believes he's going to make her rich."

"And you're not worrying about all that money Emma's given him?"

"I am worried. I really am, but if I try to discuss it with her, she gets furious with me. Her pride is at stake, Kim. I can't question Emma too closely about money. If I question her competence to handle it, I—well, I just won't do it to her. The money's not that important. If we lose it, I've still got my paycheck coming in."

"You'll never get to Greece this way," I said. "Do you know how Orlop got your name?"

"No."

"From the telephone book. He ripped the page of D's right out of the telephone book and just picked you out."

"What's wrong with looking people up in the telephone book, for heaven's sake?"

"What kind of person rips out pages from a phone book?" I demanded.

Her eyes twinkled. "Not a very considerate person."

84

"There wasn't even an address on his calling card," I persisted.

"Kim, you must admit you're prejudiced against the man. You just don't like him."

"It doesn't matter whether I like him or not. I don't want to see him ripping you off, that's all."

"Well, I'll tell you what I'll do. I'll write to the State of Virginia and see if he is a licensed genealogist there as he claims, and I'll write to that college he says he graduated from to see if he really matriculated. To be honest, I do find it hard to believe he's a college graduate. Though I suppose a college degree doesn't always remove a person's ignorance."

I sighed. "By the time you get the answers, Emma may have given him everything you own."

"Oh, stop worrying. I'm positive Malcolm wouldn't cheat Emma deliberately. My only doubt is about the reality of the inheritance."

"Then how about investigating that?"

"All right, I'll look into it. I'll even get the advice of a woman lawyer I know. Now come on, cheer up. Tomorrow's your big date, isn't it?"

"Right."

"I hope Eric doesn't disappoint you."

"Eric? He's the only bright spot in my life right now." The bell for homeroom rang. "I have your book," I said. "I wanted to talk to you about it."

"Did you like it?"

"Loved it." I was glad to be saying something nice to Ms. Davis after picking at her so much about Orlop.

"Good. Stop by this afternoon and let's talk about it. OK?"

"Right," I said. "I will." I left as her homeroom kids began piling in.

At lunch that day, Morey told me that since he hadn't yet gotten a good copy of the letter, he hadn't given it to the police.

I told him about the phone call and about Ms. Davis's conviction that Orlop sincerely believed there was a fortune to inherit. "I suppose it's possible," I said doubtfully, poking at the chicken salad instead of eating it.

"It's also possible that he could think Emma was a sweet old lady and be willing to fleece her anyway," Morey said. He gave me half of the banana bread his mother had baked and waved off my thanks.

"You do think that phone call was Orlop trying to find out if we'd given the letter to the police, don't you, Morey?"

"Probably. He's weird enough to pull a trick like that. I hope Ms. Davis is right that he's harmless."

"Morey, don't look so worried. I'm nervous enough on my own account already."

Lunch, as usual, went by faster than any other period. After we separated, I realized I'd been so concerned about myself that I hadn't even asked Morey how his magazine editors' conference had gone. Not that Morey would think anything of that. He wasn't a person who needed to talk about himself. He did things for the sake of doing them, not talking about them.

It would be nice, I thought, if he'd do something about getting Malcolm Davis Orlop out of my life.

chapter ten

As soon as I finished my private flute lesson Thursday afternoon, I rode my bike over to Ms. Davis's house. She greeted me at the door with such a pained expression that I asked, "What's wrong?"

"Emma's absolutely furious with me."

"Maybe I ought to come some other time?"

"No, no. Come on in. You're just the moral support I need."

I hung my jacket in the closet behind the door and almost bumped into Ms. Davis, who was hesitating between turning right toward the kitchen or left toward the hall where her study, her mother's bedroom and the bathroom were.

"I guess you'd better say hi to Emma," she murmured finally. "If she'll talk to you. She's not going to talk to me anymore she says."

At the kitchen, I looked over Ms. Davis's shoulder. Emma was whisking something in a bowl energetically. "Emma, we have a visitor," Ms. Davis announced.

Emma glanced our way, angry eyes magnified by her glasses and mouth drawn down to the first of her double chins.

"Hi, Emma. How are you?" I said.

She wouldn't answer. Instead, she turned her back toward us so all we could see was her curls vibrating as she whisked away.

"Mother!" Ms. Davis said. "It's not like you to act this way to a guest."

"Don't you talk to me that way, Deirdre Davis. I'm not as dumb as you think I am. I know Kim's in cahoots with you against Malcolm. The two of you think you're so smart. But what's it going to end up in? Your being done out of what's rightfully yours, that's what!"

"Emma, you're making a big fuss over nothing," Ms. Davis said. "I did not tell you you shouldn't give him more money. I only said we should wait until I checked into things a little further before handing him such a large amount."

"What things? You want to write letters asking if Malcolm's a respectable man? I don't need proof of that. I don't need everything in writing like some people I know. God gave me good sense and good judgment of people, and I use it. If you had any respect for me, you'd take my word for it. He's a fine man and a good man and his only interest is in seeing justice done."

89

"I do trust your judgment. You know I do," Ms. Davis said. "But what's so terrible if I just write to verify that what he says is so—that he is a licensed genealogist, if there is such a thing, and that a Charles Davis is a missing heir of Percy Lambreth Davis. It's just prudent to check that far, Mother. After all, he's asking for thousands of dollars now."

"Not for himself," Emma said. "He's not asking for money for himself, just what he needs to push our claim."

Ms. Davis drew a deep breath. "If the inheritance is there, it's not going to evaporate overnight."

"All these years," Emma complained, "you pretended I had charge of our money, and I believed you. But now it comes out. You don't respect my judgment one bit, Deirdre, not one bit." She sniffed back the tears.

"Mother, we just got this house paid off. Now you tell me you want to mortgage it again. We're barely keeping our heads above water as it is."

"Since when do you know anything about mortgages and debts!" Emma cried. "All these years you've acted as if you couldn't balance a checkbook. You needed me to run things, you said." Her voice rose. "Well, I've got news for you, Deirdre. This house is in my name, and if I want to borrow money from the bank on what's my own property, I will."

"Emma, you're impossible, and I'm not going to say another word to you on this subject until we both calm down." Ms. Davis grasped my wrist and dragged me off to the study. There she threw herself into the bean bag chair, punching it into shape with her elbows.

I sat cross-legged on the floor and leaned against a pile of books. Now they were talking about thousands of dollars instead of hundreds. If Orlop was a crook, if my feelings about him were right and Emma's were wrong, the Davises were headed for disaster.

"You started me thinking yesterday, Kim," Ms. Davis said. "So I began questioning Emma more closely. That man has wormed his way into Mother's affections so thoroughly he's addled her brains."

"What are you going to do about it?"

"I don't know. To take a risk like that! It's foolish, and the more I point out how reckless it would be, the more stubbornly she sticks by her decision. My mother is a darling woman, and she is also the worst person to deal with when she gets her mind set on something. *And* if I upset her, there's her high blood pressure, and her heart, and—I don't know." Her eyes went to her desk where a letter was lying opened. She picked it up and folded it back into the envelope. I saw the foreign stamps.

"Your friends in Greece?" I asked.

"One very special friend." She smiled, forgetting her concern and turning dewy-eyed. "He's a professor of Greek literature in Athens, the most sensitive man. I told you about the Greek exchange student whose family invited me to stay with them in Athens?"

"Yes."

"Well, this is his older brother."

"That's great!" I said, impressed by the way her face had turned pretty. Her cheeks flamed pink and her eyes were sparkling. I had a flash image of Ms. Davis standing in some moonlit, broken-columned Greek temple with a handsome, bearded professor at her side. "Does he have a beard?" I asked.

"A beard? No. Would you like to see his picture?"

"Love to."

All smiles, she slipped a photograph out of her desk drawer. "I'm going to buy a frame for it." She handed me the photo as if it were precious.

In the picture I saw a bald, homely, middle-aged man with a big nose and knobby knees. He was wearing shorts. They weren't becoming. "He's—" I started, trying to find something nice to say that wasn't an outright lie. "He's intelligent looking."

"He's a brilliant man. He writes the most thought-provoking letters, and yet they're so warm. We've become good friends through our letters."

"It's probably not a good photograph," I said, without thinking how it would sound.

"Kim Terrell! You're disappointed, aren't you?"

"Well—"

"Well, you are. I forget how young you are sometimes. You haven't learned the unimportance of looks yet."

92

"OK," I said. "But—" I thought of Eric. His looks were what caused all that agitation in my nerve endings. How could she say looks weren't important when they could do that to me? "Take Morey," I said. "I like him very much, and he's a good friend to me, but I couldn't imagine—you know—him and me—he and I— I mean, being together that way. I mean—"

I was saved from drowning in my embarrassment by the doorbell. Ms. Davis said, "I hope that's not Malcolm."

"Is *he* supposed to come today?"

"No, but Emma encourages him to drop in anytime and he does."

"If it's him, I'm leaving," I said. "Would you steer him away from the front door so I can sneak out?"

"I'll try." She stood up and put the picture back into the drawer. "I'll take him into the kitchen. Just wait a few minutes."

I waited behind her study door and heard Orlop say, "I'm glad I caught you in, Deirdre. You're just the lady I wanted to see. I have something to show you. Where's your young friend?"

"Pardon me?"

"Kim Terrell. I see her bike's outside."

Trapped, I stepped out of the study and joined the three of them in the living room. "Thanks for lending me the book, Ms. Davis," I said. We never had gotten around to discussing it, but that was the least of my regrets right then. "I'll see you in school tomorrow. . . . Bye, Emma." I turned and nodded at Orlop, then opened the closet to grab my jacket and run, but I wasn't fast enough.

"Kim," Emma said. "I was telling Deirdre how upset Malcolm still is about that letter he lost, and she says you found it. Why don't you give it back to him now he's here?"

I looked at Emma with horror. How could she betray me like this? "I don't have the letter now," I said.

"Where is it then?" Emma asked irritably.

"I don't have it."

"I'll be here a while," Orlop said. "You run home and get it."

"I can't." I looked at Ms. Davis for help, but she was frowning at Orlop.

"I don't understand why that letter is so important to you, Malcolm," she said.

"Just a valuable piece of information for my records," he said. "I'm a careful record keeper."

"It's *his* letter," Emma said indignantly. "He doesn't have to explain why he wants it back."

"I don't have it," I said again. "Someone else has it."

"Who?"

"I can't say."

"Kim Terrell!" Emma said. "And I thought you were such a nice girl!"

"Never mind," Orlop said. "Kim will change her mind when she hears what I have to say." He turned to me and said, "Now sit down and listen good."

I sat.

"All right then." He addressed Ms. Davis and me as if were were the jury. "What I want to do this afternoon, ladies, is put your mind at rest once and for all about this inheritance. Then I can go about getting it for you without interference." He turned toward Emma. "Right, Emma?"

She smiled encouragement, and he focused on Ms. Davis again. "Now I want you to study these papers carefully so you'll see how they pertain. Everything's here. All the important documents." He withdrew a manila envelope full of papers from his case. "Be careful with them now. They're valuable. Worth a million dollars to you in fact. More maybe." He handed Ms. Davis a newspaper clipping. "Now," he demanded, "what does that say? Read it aloud so we can all hear."

"You showed us this before," Ms. Davis said drily.

"All right. But it's important to start from the beginning so you see how it all fits together. Here, for instance, you haven't seen this yet. If you'll kindly describe it to us, Deirdre."

Ms. Davis raised an eyebrow, looking uncomfortable, but she obliged him. "This is a copy of a birth certificate that says Charles Lee Davis was born to one Anson and Thelma Davis in the year of our Lord 1920."

"And your father's uncle's name was?"

"Charles Davis."

"Charles *Lee* Davis," Emma corrected her.

"Now this," said Orlop sounding triumphant. He

passed over a folded sheet of crackling white paper.

"It's a family tree," Ms. Davis said levelly.

"And? Look there in the lower right corner and tell us what you see."

"According to this, Anson Davis was Percy Lambreth Davis's brother, which makes my great uncle his nephew. Yes, I see."

"*Now* are you convinced?" Orlop asked.

"I don't see why my father wouldn't have mentioned—"

"Family feuds," Orlop shot out. "People get such a hate against each other they refuse to mention their own kin by name. It's a common thing."

"Your father never was much of a talker," Emma said.

"But even if there is a relationship, even that close a relationship," Ms. Davis plugged on, "how can we be sure there aren't other relatives who have a better claim—"

"Now that, that is why I'm going to need some monetary support to fight this thing. No, don't for one minute imagine that they're just going to hand over your rightful due without a fight." Orlop leaned forward. "But right here, Deirdre, sits a man who will fight tooth and nail for you, for you and this dear, dear lady here." He swallowed and exchanged a tender look with Emma.

"But why does Emma have to mortgage the house?" I burst out.

"It's like an investment," Emma said.

"I don't know," Ms. Davis said. "It's a big step to take. We certainly should get the advice of a lawyer at least."

"Lawyers!" Orlop cried. "It's the shyster lawyers and the crooks at the banks that kept your inheritance from you in the first place. Out to line their own pockets, every one of them. Now, you go to a lawyer, and I have to warn you, I will no longer be interested in representing you in this case. You'll be on your own. I'll wash my hands of you."

"There now," Emma said on cue. "I told you to keep out of this, Deirdre."

"Don't be angry with her, Emma," Orlop said. "But I must make you ladies understand how confidential all this has to be."

"You're as bad as your father, Deirdre," Emma said. "Not a drop of gambler's blood in you. He never would do anything with our money except to stick what little we could save in the bank, where we never got any benefit out of it, and then at the end, didn't it all go to pay his medical bills?"

"But Mother, we're not in a position to gamble," Ms. Davis said wearily. "To go borrow more when we owe so much—"

"You never did understand money," Emma said. "Malcolm's going to make you rich, with nothing to worry about for the rest of your life."

Ms. Davis looked unconvinced. I was rooting for her to stay that way. I started biting my knuckle, waiting to see what would happen.

"It's not that I'm unappreciative of Malcolm's concern for us," she said, "but I still feel we should take some time to think it over, a few weeks at least."

"Time's just what we don't have," Orlop said. "Remember, Deirdre, I'm in this with you. I stand to inherit some of this fortune they're keeping from us, too, and I can't take the chance of losing out while you sit around making up your mind."

"Maybe it'll turn out you and Deirdre are cousins," Emma mused.

"Still and all, I don't see the urgency. It's too big a decision to make quickly," Ms. Davis insisted.

"The urgency is I have reservations on a plane out of here tomorrow. Now I don't mean to be rude," Orlop said, "but fond as I am of Emma's cooking and warm as I feel toward you both, I just can't afford any more time up here. If you folks don't want to be in on this, well, I'm sorry. I've done my best for you. It's too bad. It's really too bad. I feel for you, Emma."

"I'll have the money for you as soon as my old friend at the bank can get it for me, Malcolm," Emma said decisively.

"That's my girl! That's the spirit I like to see. I knew I wasn't wrong about you, Emma. Now, what I'll do is come by tomorrow and take you to the bank so you can sign those papers. My plane doesn't leave until evening, luckily."

"I've got to get home," I said. He was a crook.

He was going to swindle Ms. Davis and Emma out of everything they had. I had to get home and tell Morey to get that letter to the police fast.

Ms. Davis nodded absently at me and didn't urge me to stay. Emma ignored me. Orlop glanced at me and started to say something, but I had my coat and was out the door before he could complete a sentence. Why didn't Orlop go con somebody who could afford it instead of bankrupting Ms. Davis just because her mother was a little foolish?

I rode my bike home feeling hot with anger. Then I turned into our apartment project parking lot, and the anger chilled down into fear. There was Orlop sitting in his car waiting for me. I don't know how he got there without my seeing him pass me on the road.

"Come here, Kim," he said. He wasn't smiling.

I stopped short, not knowing which way to go to avoid him. I only hoped lots of people were sitting in the lit apartments watching for their families to arrive home for dinner.

"What do you want?" I kept my distance from his car.

"Go get it for me."

"I don't have it."

"You better stop fooling around. I'm tired of it."

"You tell Emma you don't need that mortgage money, and I'll get you the letter," I said recklessly.

He was leaning on his car doorframe with his head out the window and no expression on his face.

"I don't know where you get the crazy idea that I'm trying to con the Davises," he said. "Don't you want them to get rich?"

"If you're honest, why do you care if the police see that letter? It was you who called the school to find out if I'd given it to them yet, wasn't it?"

"You better give me back my letter now," he said in a voice so tightly coiled that it scared me. His hand squeezed into a fist and his eyes were blue chips again. Eerie, that he could change from bland to menacing so fast. I backed my bike up slowly, wishing I hadn't opened my mouth.

"I don't have the letter," I said. "It's in school."

"In school?"

"In my locker in school," I lied, praying my usual blush didn't betray me.

"Liar!" he said.

"I'm not lying. I swear it."

"All right. I'll give you till tomorrow. Hear me? Tomorrow. But, I'm warning you, if the police get that letter, I'll get you. I'll fix that pretty face so you won't want to look in a mirror again. You understand? Nobody does me dirt and gets away with it."

The car door began to swing open. I unfroze and raced my bike around the apartment building to the far side, where I banged on Jo Ann's door. I kept banging in a mindless frenzy until I realized that she wasn't home and he wasn't chasing me anyway.

Then I looked up at the balcony of my own

apartment and saw the light go on in our living room. I panicked, thinking he'd gone upstairs. It took the sight of a man getting out of a car in the next apartment block to make me stop whimpering and remember that it was late enough for Mother to be home. It could be her upstairs instead of Orlop.

I crept back around the building and peeked. Orlop's car was gone. Mother's was parked beside the front door. I shoved my bike inside our downstairs door and ran upstairs. When Mother asked me why I was shaking, I said I was cold and had a terrible headache. It was true. I did. Then I called Morey.

"Did you give the letter to the police yet?" I murmured, cupping the receiver with my hand so Mother, who had the radio on anyway, couldn't hear.

"I haven't had fifteen minutes free to do anything, Kim. My sister disappeared and we all went crazy looking for her."

"Did you find her?"

"Sure. She was hiding under the stairs. She's some character."

"Morey, I need the letter. Orlop threatened me. He said—he said he'll get me if I give it to the police." The threat was so ugly I couldn't repeat it even to Morey.

"You really want to return the letter to him? It's the only evidence we've got."

"I don't care. I'm so scared. Morey, he meant it."

"Then let's take the letter to the police tonight."

"No, I can't. Suppose they let him go? They could let him out on bail or something, couldn't they? And then—"

"Yeah. They could. All right, don't be scared, Kim."

"If I give him his stupid letter, he'll leave me alone."

"Yeah, right. Don't worry. I'll bring it over tonight."

"You don't have to. Mother's home with me now. I told Orlop it was in my locker at school. So as long as you give it to me first thing in the morning—"

"He say when he's coming for it?"

"No."

Mother turned the radio off and called, "Kim, are you all right? Who are you talking to?"

"Morey," I told her over my shoulder and into the phone I said quickly, "See you tomorrow, Morey." Then I hung up. I didn't want Morey riding around in the dark with Orlop on the loose. It would only take me ten minutes to run to school next morning by way of the shortcut across the fields. In bright daylight I'd be safe.

chapter eleven

Squirmy fears about Orlop kept interrupting my dreams Thursday night. I slept so badly I had an excuse for waking up late for a change. Mother had already left for work. I went dashing off to school in such a hurry that I nearly missed the note taped to our doorbell.

"Re our conversation yesterday," it read. "Hold off until I get back to you. It's possible I'll do what you suggested, but only if that property of mine remains in your possession. You know what I mean. Keep it until you hear from me as I have to go out of town."

Instead of a signature, Orlop had tacked one of his calling cards to the typed note. He must have waited until Mother left and then stuck the note on the door. I looked around the parking lot anxiously, but it was as vacant as always on a workday morning.

I read the note over four times until I had calmed down enough so it began to make sense to me. What

I had "suggested" was that he should tell Emma he didn't need the mortgage money. In exchange for which I'd return his letter. Had I really won? It would be marvelous. But the line in his note that gave me the most relief was the one about his going out of town. Maybe he'd never come back. Then the Davises would be out five hundred dollars, which is a lot of money, but they wouldn't mortgage their house, and I wouldn't ever have to see the two-faced Malcolm Davis Orlop again.

While we were studying slides of protozoa in Mr. Kramer's class, I told Morey about the deal I'd made with Orlop. "The only thing I feel bad about is that the police won't have anything to convict him with if he pulls the same thing again. I'll bet Emma isn't the only dear old lady he's been gypping."

"I made a copy of the letter," Morey said. "But I asked a lawyer friend of my dad's, and he says the police won't accept a copy, no matter how good. They'll insist on having the original."

"Well, I can't help it," I said, still thinking about Orlop's other victims. "I need the letter more than the police do."

"Don't sweat it, Kim. The letter's really too washed out and illegible to be any good as evidence anyway," Morey said.

I opened the plain white envelope into which he'd tucked the letter, and studied that famous document before stowing it in my pocketbook. The ink on the handwritten note was so blurred that I could only read one phrase— ". . . that you bring the money with you to . . ." The envelope had lost its stamp, but not the postmark and the post office stamp indicating it had been incorrectly addressed. The address was in the same smudged ink as the letter and was unreadable. Nevertheless, I felt safer having it in my purse.

All I had to do all day was keep my eyes fixed convincingly on teachers while lovely, long conversations with Eric went on nonstop in my head. As the hour for our date crept closer, I got more and more excited. Then in my French class I stopped functioning, nearly fainting as I realized Eric had never told me what time he was picking me up. In fact, he hadn't looked at me or spoken to me once since he'd invited me to go to "the game" with him. Maybe it had been some kind of joke. Maybe he had no intention of showing up tonight. Maybe— The French teacher was talking to me. "What?" I asked. "Quoi?"

"Est-ce que vous êtes malade, Kim?"

"Oh, oui," I said, glad to have an excuse to leave the room. I fled to the girls' room and looked at my stricken face in the mirror. Stop that, I told my reflection. It's not the end of the world. Even if the date was just a joke, you'll survive. But I knew I wouldn't really.

After the last bell rang, I was dragging myself down the hall to my locker when a voice said, "Pick you up around seven thirty, OK?"

My head jerked around and hinged back. "Oh, right, Eric," I said, looking up and up and up and practically melting with relief.

All the way home I smiled to myself while I sorted through my imaginary conversations with Eric for ones that I could actually use. 'Eric, you have the most fantastic eyes' was definitely out. 'Tell me all about basketball, Eric' was closer to possible. 'When did you first start playing? Do you plan to be a professional? What are you thinking about when you sit there in class staring straight ahead? How do you manage to look so innocent when you're the one who shoots all those spitballs at teachers when they're not looking?' If only I didn't go tongue-tied in his actual presence!

At seven o'clock I was bathed and dressed in my blue sweater and the only pants I had that didn't make me look too skinny. My stomach was flopping about like a newly caught fish, and Mother was buzzing in my ear about not knowing where to reach me, and why hadn't I found out what game he was taking me to. She made me so nervous that I screamed at her, and we had a fight that left us both teary-eyed and miserable.

The doorbell rang. I leaped to answer it. The guy standing on my front steps looked a little like Eric, only older and not as handsome. "I'm Eric's brother," he said. "He's waiting in the car." He gestured over his shoulder.

"Oh," I said and remembered. "Say, do you know what game we're going to? My mother would sort of like to know."

"Hockey game over at R.P.I. I used to go to college there." He was talking over my shoulder directly to my mother, who was standing on the steps behind me.

"I see," Mother said. "Well, have a nice time, Kim."

I looked back at her and blew her a kiss, a silent apology. She smiled and made a kissing motion back. Good. We'd made up and I could enjoy the evening without feeling guilty about fighting with Mother. Of course, it seemed odd that Eric hadn't come to the door himself, but I figured he probably had a good reason.

The car was a dented, rusty oldie. Eric was scooched back in the corner as far as someone his size could get. The girl in the front seat looked a lot older than me and sort of sexy. We smiled at each other, but she didn't introduce herself. As soon as Eric's brother slid into the driver's seat, she fitted herself against his side and ignored everybody but him.

"Hi, Eric," I said.

"Hi," he said looking at me and then out the window.

"I don't know a whole lot about hockey," I said.

"It's just a game," he said.

"Well, maybe you can explain some of the rules to me?"

"OK," he said.

I waited in case he had any conversational openers on hand, but he didn't say anything. All he could be seeing out the window was dark shapes and lights from cars and houses and gas stations whizzing by, not all that fascinating. Of course, he could be in a bad mood, or maybe he was shy. Was that all Eric's mystery really was? Lots of people who seem cold or distant turn out to be just shy. I warmed to the idea of getting him to open up.

"Wasn't that an awful test in social studies today?" I asked.

He turned from the window to frown at me. "Don't talk school," he ordered, fixing his eyes on the back of his brother's head. I got the message. His brother was R.P.I.—college—and we were just high school kids.

It was a long, long drive, but nobody said a word the rest of the way. When we piled out of the car in the parking lot, I overheard an interesting bit of conversation, though. Eric's brother zipped a glance up and down me and said to Eric, "So this is the one?"

"Yeah," Eric said.

I spent the first half of the game chewing that one over. Was it positive or negative? So this is the one what? The one you like? The one who stares at you in school? It shook me not to know whether to feel pleased or embarrassed.

By the second half of the game, I got interested in all those clashing sticks and flashing skates on the ice, but nobody wanted to explain to me what was happening. Not that it would have been easy to hear in the noisy stadium. The spectators really got into the action, yelling and jumping out of their seats. I would have been happy to yell too if I'd known what to yell about.

Going home was when it happened. It was so dark, I didn't even know where we were until Eric's brother pulled the car off the road, bumper up to the airport fence—our local lovers' lane.

"Uh, what are we stopping here for?" I asked.

"To watch the planes come in," Eric's brother said. He lit up a cigarette, puffed on it, and handed it to his girl, who was so welded to his side that her hair seemed to flow from his armpit. She had gorgeous black hair.

Next thing I knew, Eric lit up and was offering me a puff of his cigarette. Dumb me. It was only then I saw that they were smoking pot. I know a lot of kids do it regularly, and I have tried it, but the one time I did it made me feel dizzy and sort of out of focus. I don't like being out of focus.

"No, thanks," I told Eric.

"You don't smoke?"

"No."

"I thought maybe you did."

"Uh-uh," I said. He puffed for a while while his brother and the girl made out in the front seat. I kept sifting through conversational openers, but I was too uncomfortable to risk any of them. Then Eric put his arm around me. Uh, oh, here we go, I thought. It was one thing to dream about being in the arms of a tall, handsome boy with Genghis Khan eyes, but somehow much less appealing to be fondled by a real boy whom I still didn't know the first thing about.

Eric's arms squeezed me closer, and I could feel my bones against his. I was trying not to breathe and thinking hard. If he kissed me, OK, I decided. But more than that and I'd get out of the car, run for the airport terminal building, and call Mother to come and get me.

"Kim?" Eric whispered.

"What?" I whispered back, hoping he was finally going to talk to me so that we could start getting to know one another. But when I turned my face toward him, he mashed his mouth down against mine, scrunching his teeth against my lips so that I would have said 'ouch' if I could have said anything. When he finally loosened his hold on me, I fumbled behind me for the door handle saying, "Eric, I really don't think we know each other well enough."

"Don't talk," he said, and closed in again in a suffocating wrestling hold that I guess might have been an embrace, except that it sure didn't feel like one.

I wriggled around trying to make up my mind

which would be worse, to fight my way out of the car or to stay still and be mauled. "Please, let's go for a walk," I said when he came up for air the second time.

Eric thought that one over, staring at the top of his brother's head, which was all you could see of the couple on the front seat now. "OK," he said.

The cold night air felt wonderful. I breathed great gulps of it. "Let's go to the terminal building and get a coke," I said and added hastily, "my treat," to keep him from thinking I expected to get more out of him than the tickets he'd already paid for.

"OK," he agreed, not at all reluctant to go beyond the car as I'd been afraid he might be. As soon as we started walking, he seemed to lose interest in me.

"Eric," I asked, "how come you asked me to go out with you tonight?"

"My brother said I could go to the game if I had a date."

"Oh. . . . How come you picked me?"

"You're always looking at me in school," he said, impatient with my questions. I didn't ask him any more.

I called Mother from the terminal building to tell her we were almost home, although I wasn't sure how long Eric's brother was going to take to cover the rest of the route.

"It didn't go well, darling?" Mother must have guessed from the sound of my voice.

"Not too. I'll tell you about it later."

She told me she'd leave her party and should be home by the time I got there. When Eric and I got back to the car, I cleared my throat and, without looking at the front seat, mentioned that my mother was expecting me home soon. Eric gave me a disgusted look and then ignored me, but his brother looked up from whatever he was doing, grunted, shot Eric a dirty look and started the car. I got out of there fast when they pulled up in front of my door.

"Thanks for a lovely evening," I said to Eric, but I don't think he bothered answering me.

Mother was at the door rummaging through her bag for her keys. "What happened?" she asked when she finally found them.

"Nothing. Just he wasn't the person I thought he was."

"But nothing happened, nothing uncomfortable for you, huh?"

"Nothing happened," I assured my worrywart mother. "It was just disappointing."

"All right. It could have been worse then. At least you learned a lesson."

"I didn't learn anything, not even about ice hockey." I was feeling the letdown after my high hopes. I was feeling sorry for myself, too.

"I thought you might have learned not to judge by appearances," Mother said, giving me only half a grin in case I wasn't up to having the moral of the story rubbed in my sore psyche.

112

"All right, Mother," I said. "I get the point."

I clumped up the stairs behind her, wondering what I'd do for dream material now that I didn't have Eric, and I bumped right into her when she stopped short at the open door to the living room.

"Somebody's been in our apartment!" she cried.

We stood side by side surveying the scene. Neither of us had sense enough to think that the burglar might still be there. Everything in the living room had been dumped on the floor, pillows from the couch, endtable drawers. Even the rug was rolled back, and all our books had been tumbled out of the glass brick shelves and tossed in heaps.

"I'm going to call the police," Mother said. She dragged me back outside. We ran downstairs and around the building to Jo Ann's. "What could he have been looking for?" Mother said.

"Money," I said. "People hide money in books." Then I thought of Orlop. "The letter! I bet he didn't go away at all. I bet he just wanted to keep me from taking the letter to the police."

"What are you babbling about?" Mother asked as she rang Jo Ann's doorbell. For a change, Jo Ann was out.

While we walked over to the Spencers to use their phone, I told Mother about the note from Orlop this morning and about the meeting in the parking lot last night. She gave me a tongue-lashing for not telling her sooner.

"I'm tired of being called hysterical," I said.

"When did I ever call you hysterical? I never said any such thing."

The Spencers weren't home either, but as we turned away from their apartment, still arguing with each other, a uniformed policeman appeared.

"Anything wrong?" he asked.

"We were just trying to call the police," Mother said. "Do you work on mental telepathy?"

"No, Ma'am. We have your apartment under surveillance. I noticed your front door was open."

"Well, somebody was in there tonight. We came home and found the place ransacked."

This time they didn't call out all the police cars in the county to help them. The policeman simply had us wait downstairs in the squad car while he took his partner up with him. In a few minutes they came back and told us we could go up. The apartment was empty. They wanted a list of what was taken, but Mother couldn't find anything missing. "My typewriter's still here, and the television and the AM/FM radio," she said.

I left Mother with the police and went into my bedroom. Already depressed by the fiasco of my big date with Eric, I didn't have much emotion left over to be upset about the invasion of our apartment. I was just glad, as Mother kept saying, that we hadn't been home. But when I saw what Orlop had done in my bedroom, I almost screamed. It was so vicious.

My bed had been stripped as if he had even

114

looked under the sheets and mattresses. All the drawers in my dresser were dumped upside down. My closet had been pulled apart. But all of that was fixable. What was nasty was Roo. My faithful old friend had been slit open from his pointy face through his pouch. Half his stuffing was lying on the floor. I groaned and reached to touch him and stumbled over the broken halves of my flute. Then I screamed.

Mother made me sleep in her bed with her. Her room hadn't been much disturbed. I couldn't fall asleep, though. It was as if Orlop had ripped into my body. I felt itchy all over with helplessness. And it didn't help to have Mother moaning about not protecting me properly, and how awful it was that she left me alone so much, and how could I have been so reckless as to bargain with Orlop over his letter. I didn't tell her the letter was still in my purse. She'd have told me to give it to the police, and I had no intention of letting go of that letter while Orlop was still on the loose. It was my only sure protection.

For the first time in years, I heard Mother say, "I wish your father were here."

"What could he do that we're not doing? He would just have called the police too, wouldn't he?"

"I don't know, Kim. I just couldn't stand it if anything happened to you. I'm so afraid. And I don't know how to protect you, and I'm never home with this wretched job that all my friends think is so glamorous." She wept and I patted her back, but I couldn't fall asleep even after she finally did.

The bright sunshine scrubbed the shadows out of the living room and kitchen the next morning, but the place still looked a wreck. Mother insisted on making a huge batch of pancakes to please me. I ate a few of them to please her. I knew I should call the Davises and tell them that Orlop had ransacked our apartment, but I wasn't ready to stand up to Emma's disbelief or her telling me it was all my fault for being rude to Orlop.

"Look," Mother said, organizing the scrambled-together utility drawer as she spoke, "we don't have to do everything in one day. We'll get your bed-room back in order and then go somewhere and have a ball together this afternoon."

"What about Orlop?"

"The police are trying to find out where he's staying."

"Will they call us?"

"They said they would."

I felt limp, as if my overworked nerves were refus-ing to function altogether. I just kept sitting, twid-dling my fork around in the maple syrup while Mother whizzed through the breakfast dishes. She was in my bedroom when I started crying.

"Kim, what is it?" she asked coming out.

"My flute!"

"I'll get you a new one."

"You can't afford it."

"Sure, I can. Don't worry about it. We'll go this afternoon and buy you a brand new flute. OK?"

"Umm," I said, not feeling a whole lot better. I dragged after her into my bedroom and tried to stuff the kapok back into Roo while Mother put my chest of drawers in order. My arms felt so heavy that it was hard to move, even though it made me feel bad to let her do all the work.

"Why don't you see what you can do with your closet?" Mother said.

"Yeah," I agreed and picked up a few shoe boxes and stacked them back in place.

"Look," Mother said. "I'm not the greatest seamstress in the world, but Jo Ann makes a lot of her own clothes. Maybe she'd put Roo back together for you."

I nodded, appreciating that Mother understood about Roo even though she was always after me to grow up enough to give him away.

The police came to dust for fingerprints again and told us they hadn't been able to pick up Orlop. Emma had grudgingly told them what motel he was staying at, but he had checked out early this morning, filled his gas tank at the nearest gas station, and asked the attendant for direction to I-90. So much for his airplane tickets! I wished Sergeant Morton were on duty. Both of these men were strangers, and I wanted the comfort of someone I knew.

"Now would you mind coming down to the station to answer some questions?" one officer asked.

I did mind. I didn't want to have anything further to do with Orlop. I wanted to go get a new flute and then go to a movie with Mother or for a drive in the country and just forget Orlop and Eric both. But I went to the police station anyway.

chapter twelve

Neither my mother nor I were at our best at the police station. I was still too wrung out to do more than droop, and Mother was hyper. Her only child was being harassed, and the police weren't nearly as alarmed about it as she expected them to be. She was chewing out my old buddy, Sergeant Morton, while I sat slumped in a chair beside her.

"You mean to say, Kim *wasn't* imagining things when she was alone in the apartment the other night? Someone did come in while she was in the bathtub?"

"Correct," Sergeant Morton said. "The D.C.J.S. ran the prints we lifted from the sliding door through their computer and nothing popped up. That means the man's got no criminal record and never was in any of the services and never applied for a pistol permit. With any of those things, they'd have a card on him. But we hand-carried the prints we lifted from last night's entry over there today, and the fingerprint experts say they match. They also match prints we got from Orlop's motel room."

"My God! That man has been in our apartment twice. Why aren't you out there finding him? My daughter's not safe in her own home. Where is she safe then?"

"Kim's going to be OK, Mrs. Terrell, but we do advise you to have a dead bolt put on your door and keep a stick in the track on your sliding door. Also, Kim better not go anywhere alone for a while. Although the chances are pretty good that Orlop won't be back for a while."

"Why not?"

"It's too hot for him here right now," Sergeant Morton explained. He went on to tell us that the police were calling all the people named Davis listed in the local telephone directory to find out who else Orlop had contacted and warn them that he was a suspected con man. Even though the police still had no proof Orlop was committing fraud, they were issuing a warrant for his arrest for an assortment of crimes including burglary, criminal mischief, and larceny.

"But how is he going to know all that?" Mother asked.

"These con men are usually pretty shrewd customers," the Sergeant said. "He knows that once he makes a move, like breaking into your apartment, he'll be under suspicion. He's not going to hang around and take a chance of being picked up for questioning. He'll most likely take the money he's gotten so far and run."

"And there's nothing you can do about it?" Mother asked, looking as if she couldn't believe that.

"Well, sure. We've got the DA's office going after the guy. They'll be checking out Texas and other places to see what kind of trail he's left. If it becomes a federal investigation, we'll have an even better chance of catching him."

"And what are you going to do about protecting my daughter?"

"There's not much we can do, Mrs. Terrell, other than what we're already doing—and other than to advise you not to let her go anywhere alone for a while."

"That's not good enough," Mother complained. "I demand a twenty-four-hour watch on our apartment. Can't Kim have a bodyguard? How do you expect me to go off to work in the morning knowing my child might be attacked or—or anything." Her eyes filled and she dug into her pouch bag for a tissue.

I was sorry Mother was so upset. Now that she was rooting for me, and the police were on Orlop's trail, I was feeling comfortable again. It almost seemed like a story that was happening to someone else as I listened to the sturdy sergeant reassuring Mother.

"Kim's not in any real danger, Mrs. Terrell," he said. "Con men are rarely violent. And as for twenty-four-hour surveillance, we'd like to do it, sure, but it's just impossible. We don't have the manpower. What we can do is make more frequent spot surveillances. Our regular patrols have been checking out your apartment already. Also, if you want, we could get a locking device put on your telephone to find out where incoming calls are coming from."

"I want everything that will ensure my daughter's safety."

"Like I say, we'll do all we can. You know, if you're really worried, you ought to send Kim to visit a relative for a while."

I didn't like the sound of that, but before I could object, Morey plunked himself down in the chair next to mine. "Where did you come from?" I asked him.

"Come outside so I can talk to you," he murmured. "It's important."

I followed him out to the parking lot. "Listen," he said, "did you tell them you have the letter?"

"No. I was waiting for them to ask me about it, but apparently nobody's said anything about it to them. I had it with me last night all the time. If Orlop comes near me, I'm going to give him his letter and run."

"Right. Soon as he sees how useless it is as evidence against him, he'll leave you alone. It's too bad you didn't have it to give him Thursday night."

"Thursday night I was still worrying about Ms. Davis's money. Now I'm more worried about me."

"I'm not going to give the police the copy either," Morey said. "It's not worth taking the chance they'll insist on getting the original. Of course, withholding evidence is not only not kosher, it's a crime, but all things considered, I want you to keep the letter."

I nodded. Morey was the only one who understood. "The police don't think he's coming back," I said.

"Yeah, but you better not go anywhere alone for a while just in case he's not your ordinary, average con man. How would you like a short, dark, permanent escort?"

I sighed. I had tried a tall, blond one and that had flopped. "You can't be around all the time either, Morey. You've got too much to do."

"Nothing's as important as shadowing you, sweetheart." His Humphrey Bogart imitation was so far off it was funny. I couldn't help smiling.

"For starters, how about a movie tonight to take your mind off things?" he said.

"I don't think so, but thanks, Morey."

"Oh, come on. There's a good murder mystery over at the mall, or we could see a rerun of *Dracula* on TV."

I laughed despite myself. "Just what I need, huh?"

"I'll even take you to some soapy love story if you want."

"I don't think so."

"Well, you could come over to my house and watch the circus."

"What circus?"

"My family performing their usual."

"Not tonight, thanks."

"OK. . . . How did your big date go?"

"What big date?"

"The hoop hero last night."

I didn't even bother asking him where he'd heard about it. I just said, "Oh him, he's not much."

"I could have told you that."

I looked at Morey, standing there and trying so hard to cheer me up. He did look a little like a troll, but his brown eyes understood me better than anyone else's did, and it warmed me to think he'd drop all his own activities to play bodyguard for me. He was a good friend, as good as Francine.

"Morey," I said, "you're great."

"I know that. What else is new?"

"I'd be glad if you'd walk me home from school this week."

"It's a deal, and remember, anytime you want to go anywhere or you're going to be alone, you call me."

"I will."

The new flute was nice. Jo Ann promised to stitch Roo up as good as new, or as anyone would be after major surgery. The superintendent came and installed a dead bolt on our upstairs door and put a piece of three-quarter-inch dowling cut to fit into the track on which the sliding door ran. Mother calmed down and let me talk her out of sending me off to visit my father. I had felt like an alien from another planet the one summer I had spent in California with him and his new wife. It wasn't an experience I wanted to repeat.

As to the Davises, when I brought Ms. Davis up to date on all that had happened, she was aghast, not at the probability that she'd never see the money Emma had given Orlop again, but at the idea of Orlop breaking into my apartment. She was convinced now that he was a crook.

Only Emma still believed he was innocent. That may have been the cause of my left-over misery— that, or my feeling that Morey was right; that Orlop hadn't done with me yet.

chapter thirteen

All the police wanted me for on Monday was to help them with a composite picture of Orlop. I told Morey he didn't have to come with me, but he insisted.

"After all, it was on her way to Grandmother's house that Little Red Riding Hood met the wolf," he said.

We didn't meet any wolves, but we did meet Ms. Davis at the police station. She was coming out of the big room where court was held when it was in session.

"What are you here for?" I asked Ms. Davis.

"The police assembled all Malcolm Orlop's victims so they could warn us about him."

"You mean all *those* people believed him too?" I stared at the dozen or more people straggling out of the big room.

"To look at some of those people, you'd never think anything could be put over on them," Ms. Davis said, and she made a covert gesture at two gaunt old men who were arguing with each other. They looked like walking double negatives with their faces permanently set to 'no.'

Ms. Davis chuckled. "Would you believe those tough old birds each gave our friend Orlop more than a thousand dollars? They're brothers. They were ready to kill each other when they found out. Each one accused the other of being an old fool. The ones I felt sorriest for were that young couple with the baby there."

We watched a sad-faced pair walking out hand in hand with the baby in a canvas sling on the father's back. "Those poor kids gave him a hundred and fifty dollars," Ms. Davis said. "It was probably their next month's rent money. That man! And I gave him credit for normal human compassion."

"Where's Emma?" I asked, thinking about the bank loan for which, according to Ms. Davis, Emma had gone ahead and applied.

"She didn't feel like coming."

"Couldn't you make her?"

Ms. Davis smiled. "There's no point trying to make Emma do something she doesn't want to do."

"But suppose Orlop comes back and asks her for the money?"

Ms. Davis sighed. "The police are pretty sure he's gone to greener pastures. He certainly made a good haul around here. And from what I could gather listening to people talk, not one of them insisted on receipts or anything in writing that could be used against him. It's amazing how trusting people are."

"You don't seem particularly upset about what he took from you personally," Morey commented.

"I'm not really. Money just isn't worth getting emotional about. So long as I have a job I enjoy and people I care about—well, life is too short to spend it worrying about money."

The lilt in her voice made me suspect she had something special to be happy about. "Ms. Davis, another letter?"

"One a day lately."

"Sounds really serious."

"Possibly." Her features positively crinkled with joy.

"Did you tell Emma about the fingerprints matching?" Morey asked suddenly.

"What?" Ms. Davis asked.

"Did you tell her how Orlop broke into Kim's apartment twice? The police took fingerprints that prove it was him."

"Emma says Malcolm *couldn't* have done anything like that." Ms. Davis shrugged apologetically. "The whole thing *is* unbelievable, even to me."

"We'd better get the police to convince Emma," Morey said. "I'll go see if they make house calls." He zoomed off, leaving Ms. Davis and me to wait there in the hall for him.

"I still don't understand what Orlop was looking for in your apartment," Ms. Davis said to me. "He couldn't still be after that letter. You said it's too deteriorated to be useful as evidence against him."

"But he doesn't know that," I pointed out. "And even if we told him, he wouldn't believe it until he saw that letter himself." I thought of Morey. If we didn't turn the letter over to the police, would we end up in jail for withholding evidence? Sure, the letter was useless, but the police weren't going to be convinced of that any more than Orlop unless they saw it themselves.

"I wonder if that man's quite normal," Ms. Davis said.

I shivered. Remembering Roo and my flute, I wondered too. No, I needed that letter in case I came face to face with Orlop before the police caught him. If that happened, I'd throw the letter at him and run like crazy. Crazy! I hoped he wasn't. I hoped he was just an ordinary, run-of-the-mill con man the way the police expected him to be.

"All set," Morey said, charging back to us. "Emma's going to get a visit from the men in blue this afternoon, or from Sergeant Morton anyway."

Emma was really peeved at me. I could tell because she barely greeted me when I sat down on the piano bench next to Morey that afternoon. What's more, not a single cookie was in sight. Emma sat on a straight-backed chair with her plump ankles crossed and her knees apart as always. She was dressed up for the occasion in a gray print dress with pearls and lipstick, but though she'd dressed up, she was not enjoying herself. Her little mouth was pursed tight as she faced Sergeant Morton and Ms. Davis, who both sat on the couch.

"I don't care what evidence you have," Emma told Sergeant Morton after he explained that the fingerprints taken from the motel where Orlop had stayed matched the ones in my apartment after the break-ins. "Lots of times evidence points against a person, and it turns out the person is innocent."

"Fingerprints don't lie, Mrs. Davis. You have to understand we know now that the same man who stayed in that motel room was the one who broke into Kim's apartment."

"Malcolm is not the kind of man who breaks into apartments. Just looking at him, you can tell he's no burglar."

I watched her sitting there as straight as her cushiony body would allow. She would defend Orlop until the end because she was that kind of loyal friend. If only she hadn't fixed on him to be loyal to!

"All right, Mrs. Davis. I'm sure you're a good judge of character," Sergeant Morton said, "but in this case—well, everyone can be wrong sometimes. Right?"

She took a deep breath and shook her head in denial. "I don't know." She wasn't admitting anything.

"What you have to ask yourself," Sergeant Morton continued patiently, "is what he was doing in

Kim's apartment? He didn't take anything. But he was looking for something. Now we strongly suspect what he was looking for was a letter he thought she had that might get him in trouble with the U.S. Postal Inspection Service."

I nudged Morey. Sergeant Morton didn't know we now had the letter, but Emma did. Morey's expressive eyebrows made black, thumbs-down signs that told me to keep my mouth shut.

"You don't *know* what the person was looking for," Emma said.

"But we strongly suspect."

"And," Emma continued, "it could be that somebody using Malcolm's motel room made the fingerprints. Or suppose a burglar got in both places and poor Malcolm gets the blame. Maybe all he did was offer someone a room for the night. That would be just like him. I don't care what Kim thinks; he's a tenderhearted man."

"But Mrs. Davis—" Sergeant Morton, strong and steady Sergeant Morton, was showing signs of faltering. Emma's stubbornness was too much even for him. I glanced at Morey, who was grinning. At least someone found Emma amusing.

"Mrs. Davis," Morey put in, "how about the fee Orlop charged for registering people as heirs when legally there's no reason to pay a fee like that. How do you account for that?"

"I'm sure there's an explanation. Maybe the laws are different in Texas."

Ms. Davis tried too. "Mother, all those other Davises I met at the police station, all of them now accept that Malcolm Orlop cheated them."

"Now Deirdre, you know people will turn on their dearest friend if you give them half an excuse. It's terrible the way people will swing right around and stab someone in the back for nothing."

It was my turn. "Emma, he broke my flute in half. He got so mad because he couldn't find the letter that just for spite he broke my flute. He's not the way you think he is. He really isn't."

"I'm sorry someone broke your flute, Kim. But it's not very nice of you to go around accusing Malcolm. You didn't see him do it, did you? You know, you never did like him. He said as much to me, how you just seemed to have it in for him from the first time you met him."

"Well, but he was horrible to me right from the beginning."

"Nonsense, Kim. You just didn't like the man."

"Mother," Ms. Davis said. "What you're saying is not fair at all. You're the one who is misjudging the man, not Kim."

"The point is," Morey said, "if Orlop comes and asks you for the money you're borrowing against the house, are you still going to give it to him?"

"I prefer not to say," Emma said with dignity. "Not in this company, not right now."

Sergeant Morton groaned. "What does it take to

convince you, lady? Do we have to catch him with his hand in the till?"

"Don't you use that tone of voice to me, young man. You may be a police officer, but I'll thank you to have some respect for your elders. Now, I think I know a decent man when I meet one. That much I've learned from long years of experience." Her voice wavered on the brink of tears. "Malcolm Orlop is a good man."

"Mother!" Ms. Davis crossed the room to put her arms protectively around Emma. "It's all right. We'll talk about it later. Don't get upset. Maybe it would be best if everybody left now?" She looked meaningfully at Sergeant Morton. "Thank you," she said to him as he rose.

"If Orlop does come around again, I hope one of you ladies will call us," Sergeant Morton said.

"Definitely," Ms. Davis agreed.

"I should say not!" Emma said in a voice that had recovered strength.

Morey and I walked out with Sergeant Morton.

"Can you believe that old lady?" Sergeant Morton demanded. "What's that guy got that makes her have so much faith in him?"

"Maybe he's got her hypnotized," Morey said.

"Maybe she just can't admit she's been taken," Sergeant Morton grumbled. "I hope her daughter can keep her from giving any more money away."

I hoped so too, but I didn't expect much, not with Emma's steel-trap loyalty.

133

chapter fourteen

The next few days were normal on the surface, but a lot was going on underneath. Morey was busy checking out a hunch he'd had about a possible connection between Orlop and Eric. "Do you think it was just coincidence that Eric asked you out on the same night Orlop searched your apartment?" Morey had asked me.

I thought about it. "Well, there was a hockey game he wanted to go to that night," I said. Still, anything was possible. Morey said he'd do some investigating and get back to me.

I walked around school attending classes, missing baskets in gym, doing all the usual things, but I was unsure of where I stood on some basic questions. It was like walking blind on patches of ice.

Take what happened at lunch on Wednesday. I sat with school friends, the kind of girls I just don't think of calling when school lets out even though they're nice kids. I was taking a bite of my cold pizza when Maryanne, who isn't the brightest girl but is good-natured, said to me, "Doesn't it bother you that Morey's so short?"

I chewed, swallowed, and said, "Why should it bother me?"

"Well, I mean, it just looks funny. I mean, you being so tall and him being so short."

"Why, Maryanne?" Liz, our group's militant feminist took over for me. "Would it look funny to you if Morey were tall and thin and Kim were short?"

"No," Maryanne said. "Boys are supposed to be taller than girls."

"Why?" Liz shot at her, leaning over the table as if she were ready to grab Maryanne by her plump throat. Luckily, Maryanne doesn't read body language too well.

"It just seems that way to me," Maryanne said and looked at the rest of us. "Doesn't it seem that way to you girls?"

"I can't believe you still think like that! You're just repeating your mother's worn-out garbage," Liz cried, eyes flashing. "Don't you realize what you're saying? There should be a big, strong man and a small, weak woman depending on him for protection . . . 'Oh, brave sir, please save me from the wolves!' . . . Maryanne, there aren't any more wolves to kill, and if there were, we women could figure out how to kill them ourselves."

"All I said was that it looks funny," Maryanne said calmly.

Liz turned a deep shade of plum. "Lord preserve me from such stupidity!"

"Liz Hambleton, I am not stupid!" Maryanne said.

I finished my pizza while they argued with each other and the other girls tried to mediate. What I was thinking was: A. Was everybody assuming that Morey and I were boy-girl friends instead of just friend-friends? B. Suppose they were. Could we be? And—biggest of all—C. Did I agree with Maryanne or Liz?

Later I was in the school lobby, staring out the big entrance window wall at the last leaf fluttering on the skinny branches of the bush outside. It was my ten-minute breather before French. Morey pulled up beside me and sat down on the tile floor with his back against the glass. "Found out anything yet?" I asked him.

"You mean Eric? I'm going to interrogate him today in gym."

I sighed.

"So how come you're so glum?" he asked.

"Thinking about Ms. Davis," I lied. "It must be frustrating having to deal with a mother like Emma. I mean, she's kind-hearted and a great cook, but so unreasonable."

"All parents are unreasonable, often irrational too. Take my mother. You know what she expects me to do?"

"What?"

136

"She expects me to take a shower without getting the floor wet. Now if that isn't unreasonable and irrational, I don't know what it is—especially since my little sister cut a window in the shower curtain so she could see out."

I laughed. "She didn't!"

"Sure, she did. She's very logical, not too clever yet, but logical. Hey, Kim, how would you like to go to a Halloween party with me?"

"A Halloween party?"

"Yeah. A Hebrew School friend of mine invited me. It'll be an old-fashioned-fun kind of thing with apple ducking and costumes. You know, just good, clean fun."

"Sounds great."

"You'll go with me?"

"Well. . . ." I hesitated, not sure I wanted to go with him, and yet, sure I didn't want to hurt his feelings. "Suppose I check with my mother and let you know?"

"OK. Meet you at the front door after eighth period. I've got to go or I'll be late for gym." I watched him charging down the hall. Someday I'd have to ask him how he felt about being short. If I were a boy, I'd hate to have to look up to everybody. Morey and me? It would be sort of like pairing a giraffe with a little bull, awkward to say the least. I had an awful lot of Maryanne in me. Liz would be disgusted. On the other hand, the boy she went with was in college, and was tall and handsome too.

137

I sighed and tried to imagine kissing Morey. The idea wasn't exactly thrilling, not the way I'd thought it would be with Eric, not even in my imagination. In fact, I couldn't quite figure out the position. Would I bend down or would he stand on a chair? Ridiculous. I was glad nobody could see what I was thinking.

That day the French teacher had to cut class short because she was feeling nauseous. I wandered down the hall to Ms. Davis's room. She was just about to get on a chair to erase the top of her chalkboard.

"Let me do that for you," I said.

"Oh, hi, Kim. Come on in." She handed me the eraser. "It must be nice to be so tall. Do you like it?"

"My height?" I asked. "It's OK. You get to stand in the back of the line and people think you're older than you are, which is nice sometimes. I'm only five eight anyway, which isn't so tall that I feel like a giant."

"No, it's a nice height."

"If I were five five though, life would be simpler." I finished erasing and looked at Ms. Davis. The gray in her suit was bringing out the gray in her hair. She looked tired.

"Morey?" Ms. Davis asked.

"Morey. Do you think height should matter?"

"It shouldn't. Chemistry is what matters. How's your chemistry with Morey?"

"I'm not sure."

"It's a problem," Ms. Davis said. "I remember a boy I went out with. He stuttered. It embarrassed me. I don't know whether it was just the stuttering—I hate to think I was that callow—or if the chemistry was wrong between us, but anyway, that's something nobody can decide for you."

I nodded, no more clear on how I felt than before. "Did you bring Emma around?" I asked, to change the subject.

"Not really. We went over and over the same arguments until I ran out of breath. I'm just going to have faith that Orlop won't come back."

"You can't influence her at all?"

"Occasionally I can. But this time she's invested so much already. I don't think she can bring herself to admit she's thrown away that much. It's more tolerable for her to see herself as a lone fighter for a lost cause."

"I see what you mean. Ms. Davis, why don't you use the money Emma borrowed on your house to get your car fixed and go to Greece?"

Ms. Davis's mouth twisted up at one corner. Suddenly I wondered just how old she was. If Emma was in her sixties, Ms. Davis could be older than my mother. Maybe this Greek college professor was Ms. Davis's last chance at romance.

"Do you know what a fatalist is, Kim?" She asked me.

"Somebody who believes life is going to turn out a certain way no matter what they do."

"Right. Well, I'm something of a fatalist about Greece, about a lot of things."

"But—" I didn't like her saying that— "that's not a good thing to be."

"For sure it's not," Ms. Davis admitted. "Lots of things I admire couldn't have been brought about by fatalists—like the American Revolution and freedom for slaves and winning women's rights. It's necessary to struggle to change things or nothing will ever be better. I know that. That's why I admire our friend Morey so much. He's always in there fighting. But I can't help the way I'm built."

I didn't agree with everything she had said, but the bell rang and ended the discussion. I went off frustrated. Ms. Davis admired Morey. I admired him too. The way he plowed in and changed things in our school was exciting. He'd been the one who set up the debates on students' rights and responsibilities. From that had come lots of things, including the peer counseling program that other schools were copying now. Morey was really quite a guy, and I thought how lucky I was that he liked me, as I pulled on my white socks for gym. Of course, that didn't tell me whether I had a chemistry problem or not, and I still wasn't sure how important height really was to me.

That night, before I called Morey to find out what he'd learned from Eric, I asked Mother if she'd let me go to a Halloween party with Morey. "Sure," she said. "Why not."

140

"But I'm not sure I ought to go with him." I wanted guidance, not calm acceptance.

"Why wouldn't you want to go with him?"

"Well, so far we've just been friends. But if we go to the Halloween party, it'll be different. We won't be friend-friends anymore. Chemistry gets involved."

"Oh?"

"Don't you have any advice on the subject?" I prodded.

"Of chemistry? I would say, don't give it a thought. He only asked you to go to a party, not to marry him."

Sometimes Mother can exasperate me. "But, Mom, suppose he expects me to feel a certain way about him and I can't?"

"Do you know how you feel about him?"

"Not exactly."

"Then wait until you do know, and if it's different from the way he feels toward you, you'll tell him then." She tasted the soup in the pot I was stirring and added salt. I stirred some more and tasted it too. As usual, she'd made it too salty.

"But suppose I hurt his feelings," I said.

"He'll recover."

"Mom, that's heartless."

"Nonsense. It's sensible. You can't prejudge relationships. You have to try them on for size."

"Size is the whole problem."

"Well, darling, I don't know what else to tell you.

If you aren't attracted to him because he's so much shorter than you, don't go out with him."

"But I'm not sure." I poured the soup into bowls and we sat down to eat.

"Then go out with him and see how the evening goes. What have you got to lose?" she asked me.

"A good friend."

"Well, maybe. Look, you know what to do a lot better than I know what to tell you in this situation. You're much less bound by convention than I was at your age. I was such a cowardly little conformist. That's why I fell for your father. He was everything my girl friends admired, and I was so flattered that he chose me. It never occurred to me to ask myself if he was what *I* wanted."

She took a spoonful of soup. "You're much more of an individual than I was, Kim. I'm proud of the way you set your own standards and walk your own path. I wish I had half your independence." She was so carried away by her own oratory that there were tears in her eyes.

I finished my soup. Even though I don't take Mother's praise too seriously, it makes me feel good. It's comforting to have your own private fan club, even if your mother is the only member.

After dinner, I called Morey. As soon as he picked up the receiver, I asked him, "Did you corner Eric?"

"Yup. I was professionally sneaky. I told him I had a message from Orlop. Eric didn't even blink. 'Who?' he asks me. So I describe Orlop and say it's

142

a very important message. 'You're crazy,' Eric says. 'I don't know any guy like that.' He was pretty convincing, Kim. I think my hunch was wrong. Eric didn't have anything to do with the break-in."

That suited me fine. "OK," I said. "Listen, Morey, about your invitation, I'd like to go." I'd decided to go finally because it made no sense not to. As Mother had pointed out, I wasn't committing myself to anything more than an evening with him.

"Great," Morey said. "I'm glad. Now what about costumes?"

"Must we?" I asked.

"Sure. That's half the fun. How about us going as beauty and the beast? My mother has an old fur coat she'd let me borrow."

I winced. Didn't he have any vanity at all? "Morey," I said cautiously, "do you think that's a good idea?"

"Yowrf," he barked or growled or whatever.

What do you do with a character like him? I tried another angle. "Well, I have a conical hat with a veil hanging from it. I wore it in the chorus last Christmas. It makes me look about ten feet tall." I was deliberately fishing for his reaction.

"Yeah, I remember that hat and that long purple dress. You looked terrific."

"It was mauve, not purple."

"Whatever. Yeah, wear that."

I nodded to myself. Obviously, the difference in our sizes didn't mean a thing to him. I was the only one with the height hang-up. As a matter of fact, if Morey had any hang-ups, I haven't discovered them. He's got a rubber-ball personality. I can just see him bouncing his way through life, never letting anything get him down.

He wound up our conversation by telling me the date and time of the party, and he made me write down the name and address of my host so I could leave it for my mother. He was considerate too; there was just no end to his virtues. I went to sleep in a happy mood.

chapter fifteen

Before I left for school the next morning, the telephone rang. I wiped the milk off my lip and answered it. Mother had already left for work. I was alone in the apartment.

"Do you still have the letter?" I flinched at the man's voice. "You didn't give it to anyone, did you?" Orlop!

"No," I whispered.

"All right. Then we'll make the exchange we talked about."

"What?"

"You know," Orlop said impatiently. "The exchange. Now listen, leave the letter under the first stone on the path between the field and your apartments. Then I'll keep my end of the bargain."

"When do you want me to leave it?"

"Now."

"But—"

"But what? Listen, you better not make me mad at you. Leave it under the first stone. Understand?"

I inhaled and was ready to say "Yes," but he hung up. I sat down. I was right back in the danger zone again. But all I had to do was leave the letter as he'd said. Or was that all? Suppose he picked up the letter and went to Emma's for the rest of his money, and she told him about the police being after him because of me. What would he do then? Leave town with the money or come after me first and then leave town? Either way was bad news. Besides, I was scared. I couldn't just leave the letter and hope for the best. I wanted protection. When I stopped trembling enough so that I could dial, I called the police.

Wouldn't you know, I was thinking as I waited for the phone to ring at the station, this was the first morning Mother hadn't made me get up early so she could drive me to school. We had just about decided the police were right and Orlop wasn't coming back. Just my luck. "Can I speak to Sergeant Morton, please?" I asked.

The officer told me Sergeant Morton hadn't come in yet. "Can I do anything for you?"

"Well," I quavered, not sure how far back in the story to begin. "This is Kim Terrell." He knew who I was. I said that Orlop had just called me and wanted me to leave the letter out for him.

"How come you didn't turn the letter over to the police?" he asked.

"It's too damaged to be any good as evidence

really," I said, trying to excuse myself. "And I needed to keep it as protection sort of because—well, just because of what happened this morning. I mean, Orlop wants that letter, and the only way I can get him off my back is to give it to him."

"You should have discussed it with us, not made that kind of judgment yourself," the officer scolded. I liked Sergeant Morton much better. Finally, he said, "OK. Wait half an hour, and then leave it where he said."

"But I'm already late for school, and besides Orlop said to leave it now."

"You've got to give us time to get there. Don't worry. He'll wait."

"Get here?"

"Right. We'll set up a lookout where we can nab him when he goes for the letter."

"But he'll see you."

"No, he won't. You leave that to us. Just wait half an hour, and then leave the letter and forget the whole thing."

I didn't like it. First of all, I felt exposed being alone in the apartment. Suppose Orlop was waiting downstairs and got impatient and came up after me! Second, if he found out I'd called the police, he'd be furious, and I didn't want Orlop getting even a little annoyed with me, let alone furious. I had my hand on the phone to call my mother at work, but I didn't dial. Why make her frantic? She couldn't do anything except rush home. By the time she got here, I'd have stuck the stupid letter under the stone and be halfway to school—hopefully.

I jittered around watching the clock for twenty-five minutes. When the phone rang again, I leaped up screaming. Luckily no one was around to notice my hysterics. To answer or not to answer? Suppose it was Orlop wanting to know why I hadn't left yet? Suppose it was Orlop telling me, never mind, he'd come and get the letter in person. It *could* be the police. Maybe it was just somebody trying to sell home rug cleaning or insurance. Gingerly I picked up the receiver.

"Kim?"

"Morey!" I cried, recognizing his voice. "Thank God, it's you!"

"Why aren't you in school? I sneaked out of Kramer's class to call."

"Orlop called," I said breathlessly. "He wants me to leave the letter under a stone. I called the police. They said to wait and then do it. I have to leave this minute."

"Are you home? I'm coming right over."

"But Morey, you don't have to—" He hung up. It reassured me knowing he was on his way. I stalled for another five minutes to give Morey time to start across the fields. Breathing deeply, I tried to relax but bits of my mind kept flying off, and I had to go to the toilet twice.

148

At 8:27 I started downstairs to do my rock bit, locking the doors behind me and looking around anxiously. A perfectly normal morning. Innocent blue sky overhead, crunchy brown leaves underfoot, empty parking lot because everyone had gone to work. No Orlop and no police in sight. Nothing to worry about. But I walked toward the path on legs about as steady as a newborn colt's. As soon as I shoved the infamous letter under the first flagstone, I dashed over the rest and sprinted across the field to meet Morey who was running toward me.

"You OK?" he gasped.

"More or less," I said.

We jogged back toward school. Only Mr. Milton, the head custodian, was in the hall as we came through the front door. Everybody else was in classes. Mr. Milton and I greeted each other while Morey gulped some water from the fountain just outside Kramer's room. Then we ducked in.

"You're late!" Kramer said. At long last he'd noticed!

"Late?" Morey said. "I'm in the middle of an experiment, Mr. Kramer. I just stepped out for a drink."

"Oh?" Kramer glanced uncertainly at the counter top where Morey and I always worked. "You're supposed to let me know when you leave the room, Stern." His gruff act didn't begin to be convincing.

"I'm sorry. Won't do it again," Morey said.

Then Kramer looked at me. I swallowed, ready to tell him I'd overslept, but he just nodded at me. "Better get back to work," he said.

"Home free," Morey whispered to me. It was over. I felt an enormous relief, and I was so tired that even though it was only 8:35, I couldn't wait for the day to end so I could fall into bed.

My belief that everything was all right now, and Orlop wouldn't bother me anymore lasted until I got home that afternoon. Mother was there waiting for me. The police had called her and told her what had happened.

"Why didn't you call me this morning?" she demanded.

"I figured there was nothing you could do, and I didn't want you to worry."

"But Kim, I'm your mother. *I'm* supposed to take care of you. Will you please stop doing the protecting around here?"

"Anyway," I said cheerfully, "it's all over."

"No, it's not."

"What do you mean?"

"Sergeant Morton said your Mr. Orlop never showed. They waited in the corner apartment nearest to the footpath all day, and he never came. Your letter stayed put until they picked it up before they left this evening."

"But— Maybe Orlop saw them?"

"I don't think so, Kim. They didn't come in a police car, and they didn't park where Orlop could

150

see them. I'm sure they took precautions. They said nobody even went near the path except some kids."

"So now what?"

"So now, I'm going to do what Sergeant Morton says would be best. I'm calling your father and telling him you're coming for a visit—a long visit, maybe a month or two. That should give the police enough time to catch this criminal or at least for him to lose interest in you."

"But what about school?"

"They have schools in California—or so I've heard."

"Mother, don't make me go. I don't belong in California. Couldn't we at least wait until after the Halloween party to decide?"

"No, you'll leave tomorrow. I can't stand any more of this."

I could see by the depth of the distress lines on her face that there was no sense arguing with her. But the thought of spending a month with my father and his new wife was a dismal prospect. Last year he came East on a convention trip, and I spent a whole day with him. We had practically nothing to say to one another. I mean, he took me out for lunch, and we talked, and then we went for a walk together, but by the end of the afternoon, I had a headache from trying to think up things to ask him. He's a nice man, but all he's really interested in is his real estate business. He even asked me about house sales in our area. As if I'd know the first thing about it! He asked me about school too, but he didn't listen to the answers. A month with my father would be deadly.

I picked up the copy of *Jane Eyre* I was supposed to be reading for English, but I couldn't concentrate even though I'd found it interesting enough yesterday. I'd have plenty of time to read on the plane to California. Five minutes later Mother plunked down on the couch beside me. I already knew I was safe. I'd heard her end of the phone conversation.

"Well?" I asked.

"He and his wife are on a trip to Hawaii. Her mother is with their children. I told her you could help take care of the kids, but she didn't sound very welcoming. I said I'd call her back tomorrow. Meanwhile we'd better think of somewhere else you could go. How about Francine?"

"Washington? Yipee! I'll call her."

"Just don't spend all night on the phone. Remember it's long distance."

Francine was thrilled to hear from me, but when I asked her if she could take me in because I needed a hideout, she asked if I'd had the chicken pox. Her little brother had come down with it.

Mother groaned when I relayed the information to her over my shoulder. "You can't go there," was all she said.

I spent another couple of minutes on the phone with Francine and promised to write and explain everything that had happened to me.

152

"Mom, I'm going to that Halloween party with Morey on Friday," I announced after I hung up. I had a hunch that the party would be a kind of test of how I really felt about Morey, and I was determined to go. As to Orlop, maybe he'd decided to let the letter disintegrate all by itself under the stone, or maybe the police had scared him off. I hoped he wasn't harboring any hard feelings against me either way. I'd tried to give him back his letter. It wasn't my fault the police took it—not much my fault anyway.

"I don't like it," Mother said. "We can't be sure that man is out of your life for good."

"Don't worry," I said airily. "Nothing could possibly happen to me now." I even believed what I was saying. Maybe Ms. Davis's fatalism was rubbing off on me after all.

chapter sixteen

Being one of a group of people all wearing the same ridiculous costume is nothing like seeing yourself in a full-length mirror and knowing you're going to be the only one at a party who's dressed that way.

What I looked like in my shapeless mauve gown with a white veil hanging from the peak of my dunce's cap was a pencil with a pointed eraser at the end. Without the hat, I didn't even look as if I were wearing a costume, unless it was a mauve shroud, and with the hat on, I went back to looking like a pencil.

"Mom, do you think makeup would help?" I asked uncertainly. I loathe makeup.

"You don't need any with your skin. Your coloring is so lovely, Kim." She came close and looked at me critically. "Maybe just some eye makeup. That mauve is not your best color."

"Forget it. I'll wear the eye mask."

"You're positive now that Morey's father is going to take you *and* bring you back?"

"Right to the door. Never fear. Morey takes good care of me." I slipped on the black mask. It helped. Now I looked like a pencil in disguise.

"But suppose I fall asleep before you get home," Mother worried. "I'm so bushed I can barely keep my eyes open now."

"Mother, what are you worrying about? Even if you're asleep, I'll be fine."

"I think what I'll do is set the alarm for midnight. Then if I fall asleep, I can be sure to wake up and check on you. You'll be back by midnight, won't you?"

"Oh, for sure. The kid's parents will kick us out long before. Mom, it couldn't be safer. Please don't worry."

Mother groaned. "This Orlop is driving me up a wall. It's getting so I'm anxious whenever you're not standing right next to me. If only they'd catch him and stick him in jail!"

The doorbell rang. "I'll get it," I said and ran downstairs with the bag of candy bars we were handing out to the trick-or-treat kids. Two kindergarten-sized ones were at the door in ghost costumes. At least, I think they were wearing ghost costumes. It was hard to tell with their bulky winter jackets covering them.

"Is it cold out?" I asked.

"Freezing. What are you dressed up for?"

155

"A party," I said.

"You look good," the littler one said.

"Thanks. So do you."

"Aw, this sheet ain't much. My good costume got busted at school."

"That's too bad. What was it?"

"I was a gumball machine."

They dumped the candy bars into their half-full shopping bags and scooted away to the next door. A gumball machine! Now *that* would have put some curves on me! A car passed with a man at the wheel. I shuddered and slammed the door shut, even though the shape of the head was not Orlop's. Mother wasn't the only one who was nervous.

I had been checking with Ms. Davis daily to find out if Orlop had contacted Emma or her. He hadn't. It still puzzled me that he had not come for his precious letter. I suspected the police hadn't been as hidden as they said they were. But something might have happened to Orlop before he got here, I thought, as I ran back upstairs. Whatever it was, I hoped it was something permanent.

The eighth time I clambered down to open the door, a squat, furry creature with a deep voice said, "Hi, or rather, yowrf. How do I look?"

"Morey! I thought you were a trick-or-treater. You look beastly."

"Good. I'll tell you, though. I'm glad I'm not a fur-bearing animal. These coats are hot."

"Come upstairs and say hi to my mother."

Mother was sitting in front of the TV calming herself with a dish of chocolate ice cream with hot fudge glopped all over it. The more unnerved my mother gets, the more sweet things she eats. If Orlop didn't disappear from my life soon, she was going to need a whole new wardrobe a size larger.

I got my hat while Morey and Mother exchanged pleasantries. "You won't let her out of your sight, Morey, will you?" Mother asked.

"I'll protect her with my life on my honor as a good beast."

The party was in the basement of a very nice house. It was a good place for a Halloween party since only the floor and one wall had been finished off, and the rest was standard, indestructible basement with pipes and cinder blocks. The kids were mostly familiar to me from school, the kind who do their homework, care about marks and stay within the rules. Nobody was about to pretend that kid stuff was beneath them or that they were too cool to laugh and run around playing games. Everybody seemed relaxed and out to have a good time. Morey and I got a lot of compliments on our paired costumes except for one wise guy.

"Who's the beauty and who's the beast?" he wanted to know. Some people think they're so funny! I hate would-be humorists like him.

Later in the evening, after the apple ducking and the balloon stomping and the harmless body contact games, like where a boy and girl are tied up together and have to escape, we were sitting quietly listening to music and drinking cider and talking. The self-appointed funny boy came over to heckle us.

"Hey! You know, you two didn't need costumes at all. You could've come as the Odd Couple."

"You think I look like Walter Matthau?" Morey asked calmly.

"Yeah, but he's taller. Yeah, I'd say you two have really got a problem."

"None that I know of," Morey said. He had discarded his fur coat, and I'd taken off my dunce cap! We weren't really even in costume anymore, and I couldn't see why this kid was still baiting us. It was annoying me, which I guess was just what the kid wanted. Morey didn't lose his cool, though.

"Yeah, you two got a problem. You can't even make out without her bending way down."

"We don't have any problem at all," I said. I don't know what got into me then, but the kid was such a pest. "See, this is how we do it." I lay back across Morey's lap and closed my arms around his neck, turning to grin at the heckler.

"Well, since you're in position," Morey said. I turned my head to find out what he was talking about, and he kissed me. Right on the mouth. Nicely. I mean, it was a nice, firm, warm, soft kiss. His arms were supporting my back like a hammock. We sort of hung there for a minute, enjoying ourselves until I remembered we were being watched.

"Hey!" I said and sat up. Would you believe my heart was racing and my cheeks felt hot?

"You started it," Morey said.

"I'm not complaining," I assured him.

"Neither am I."

It was a fantastic party. We ended up talking in the kitchen with Morey's friend David, who is a really brilliant guy—you know, the kind who takes college courses during his summers between high school terms and ends up at Harvard. The conversation was about whether a religion had to include a belief in God or not. Ms. Davis had been talking about karma to one of her classes, and some kids had the idea that that was her religion.

David said, "Karma isn't a religion. It's just a belief that what a person *is* determines his fate in his next life. A religion is a set of beliefs about who we are, where we come from and where we're going."

"Religion's just a way of answering questions that people really don't know the answer to," Morey said.

"You mean, you don't think religious beliefs come from God?" David asked him.

"Like Moses and the Ten Commandments?" Morey asked.

"Along those lines. Most religions claim to have been handed down to man from some supernatural being."

"Can you be a Jewish atheist?" Morey asked joking.

"I suspect you are one, Morey."

"Me? You know I'm a good Jewish boy, David. You went to my bar mitzvah."

"But what you said," David, the future professor pointed out, "proves you think God is an idea man made up."

I listened to them arguing back and forth, fascinated, but having a hard time following because my mind wandered off. I started wondering where my own stand on religion was. I mean, I believe in God sort of, but not in a particular personal god. I have this feeling it's not so much what he can do for me, but what I'm supposed to do, like trying to be a better person and caring about other people's needs.

It's frustrating the way I run into this cloud of unfinished ideas whenever I start thinking about what I really believe about something. According to Mother, it doesn't get any better either. She says she discovers more questions she doesn't have the answers to all the time. I hope that's not the way it will be for me. I like answers.

"I need to do a lot more of that," I told Morey later when we were waiting for his father to pick us up.

"More of what?"

"Talking about important things."

"You didn't say anything."

"Well, I was thinking. I need to get my ideas sorted out. I wish I could be around for more discussions like that."

"Whew!" he said.

"Whew, what?"

"I was afraid you were bored."

"I'm never bored with you," I said.

He hugged me affectionately. It felt natural to be hugged by Morey and very nice. Just then his father pulled up and honked his horn at us. We got into the back seat.

"How was the party?" his father asked.

"Good," Morey said. "We ducked for apples and discussed the theory of religion."

"Sounds like a well-rounded affair," Morey's father said. He looked a lot like Morey, only a few inches taller and with a mustache.

"Say something," Morey told me, squeezing my hand.

"I had a good time," I said.

"How about when that nerd Eddie was needling us?"

"That turned out all right."

"I thought it turned out great," Morey said. "Maybe I'll hire him to come bug us next time we go somewhere together."

It occurred to me that Morey wasn't as uniformly self-confident as I'd thought. He wasn't going to come right out and tell me that he liked me, but he did like me. It was odd to think of funny, outgoing Morey being even the least bit unsure of himself. Probably there was a lot I didn't know about him.

"You don't need Eddie," I said. "You do just fine without him."

161

"I do? You mean the beast turned into a handsome prince like in the fairy tale?"

"Well, let's not go that far."

"Ah hah! You mean, it's going to take more than one kiss to transform me?"

"Down beast, down," I said.

Mr. Stern parked right next to my door. A white van was parked on the other side. Mr. Stern was grinning when he opened the car door for me. I guessed he'd been listening to us, but I didn't mind.

"Thank you very much for driving me, Mr. Stern," I said.

"And thank you, Morey, for a great evening."

"When you get upstairs," Morey said, "blink the lights in your room twice so we'll know you're all right."

I looked up at the bedroom windows. They were dark. Mother must be asleep. "Morey, don't be silly. My mother's home."

"OK, but do it anyway," he insisted.

I made a face at him and got my key out to unlock the door, glancing at the white van as I turned. Nobody but visitors ever parked where that van was, but nobody would be visiting us this late. It was probably one of Jo Ann's friends who'd parked on the wrong side of the building. Ridiculous to be uneasy, I thought. I'm home. Orlop hadn't come for the letter, but that wasn't my fault. He wouldn't be after me now. I finally got the key to work, waved one last time at Morey and his father, and stepped inside. I glanced up the staircase, flipped on the light switch, waved again and closed the door behind me.

There he stood, not a shadow, not a dream, but terrifying reality. Orlop, leaning against the wall behind the door and looking at me. I opened my mouth to scream. He lunged toward me and wrapped a gag around my face. Then he pinned me to the wall with the weight of his body while he tied the gag. I tried to scratch his hands loose, but he finished and grabbed my wrists and tied them behind my back.

I was helpless, limp with fear, when he turned me to face him and warned in a whisper, "Be quiet now. Nothing's going to happen to you if you keep quiet. All I want's the letter. You understand? I'm not going to hurt you. Not unless you make me nervous. You understand?" He shook me. "Nod your head."

I nodded.

"OK. Now listen. Are you going to cooperate with me this time? You going to get the letter for me? Then we'll be even, and I can get out of here for good. All right?" He shook me and I nodded again.

His eyes studied me suspiciously. "You going to scream when I untie the gag? You scream and I'll have to shut you up fast. You understand?" He showed me his fist and pretended to ram it in my face.

I ducked and he grinned. "Yeah, you're smart.

163

Too smart, butting in where you don't belong. If you'd left that letter where I told you, we'd be quits by now. When the kid came back and told me there wasn't anything under that stone, I wanted to hit you so bad."

He shook me in anger. With the gag in my mouth, I couldn't say a word. All I could think was that he had sent a kid instead of going for the letter himself, and that's why the police hadn't seen him. But why hadn't the kid found the letter? I'd put it where Orlop said. My eyes filled with tears from the pain of the gag and ropes eating into my flesh, and from fear.

"Don't cry," he said. "That's not going to do us any good. Don't cry."

I opened my eyes as wide as I could, trying to control the tears while he frowned at me.

"Got to take a chance," he said. "We can't stand around here all night." He glanced at the door at the top of the stairs.

Oh, Mother, wake up and come help me I begged inside my head. Where should I tell him the letter was? If I told him the police had it, he might hurt me just to punish me. I didn't want to give him an excuse. Tell him it was upstairs? He was untying the knot. I could hear his breath coming hard and the banging of his heart, or was that my own?

"One sound," he was muttering. "You make just one sound and you'll regret it."

Being free of the gag was a relief. I swallowed drily.

"OK.," he said. "Tell me quick where you hid it." He glared at me with hatred in his eyes.

"You didn't come for it," I said. "I left it under the first stone just like you said. Why didn't you pick it up?"

"Liar," he whispered and his lips twisted. I ducked, thinking I was about to get it. "Stop that," he said, pinching my shoulder. "Stop your lying. I sent a kid to pick it up. Paid him five dollars and five more if he came back with it. He didn't find anything."

"But I left it under the first stone just like you said." I pointed as if we could see the path through the closed door. All at once I understood what might have happened. "The first stone at this end of the path. Maybe the kid looked under the first one from the field end."

I held my breath while he thought that over. "Then where is it now?" he asked.

I hesitated, swallowing another dry swallow, trying to think fast.

Just then the alarm rang. It vibrated shrilly through the closed door at the top of the stairs. Orlop flipped off the light switch and covered my mouth with his hand. In the dark I could hear the scuffling of Mother's slippers. I remembered she'd said she would set the alarm for midnight. Now she was checking to see if I was home.

"We've got to get out of here," Orlop whispered. He tugged open the door and pulled me out after him. The only free part of me was my legs, so I tried to use them. I stuck out a foot to trip him at the step, but all that earned me was a slap. "Little troublemaker," he snarled and dragged me toward the van.

"It's still under the stone, the first stone," I said desperately, wresting myself free of his hand long enough to blurt that out. No way did I want to end up in the van with him.

"Whyn't you say so?" He didn't wait for an answer. He half dragged, half walked me through the parking lot toward the path to the fields. I could hear my heart drumming wildly as I tried to think what to do when he didn't find the letter where I'd said it would be. Would he beat me up? Kill me? Morey, I screamed inside my head. Why didn't you check up on me like you said? He'd told me to turn on the lights and I hadn't. Why did he just go home then?

"This is it," Orlop said. "OK, which stone? This first one?" He bent to turn the flagstone over, but the *varoom* of a car charging our way made us both look up. It was startling because the headlights were off.

The car yanked to a stop beside us and the doors flew open. At once Orlop let go of me. He raced off toward the field, but a short, dark shape was right on his tail. Morey! He tackled Orlop midway up the path. Orlop went down, and Morey's father lent his weight to the task of keeping him down. Then a police car zoomed through the parking lot coming from Van Worth Road. It skidded to a stop inches from the Sterns' car doors.

Orlop was yelling, "I didn't touch her. I didn't do anything. Let me go."

"Sit on his head, Morey," Mr. Stern growled. Two hefty policemen bounded up the path to the rescue.

"Hey, are you all right?" It was Morey's deep voice at my ear.

"Hi, prince," I said. He was trying to untie my wrists. "I'm fine. I think." I was shaking so hard my teeth chattered.

When Morey got the rope untied, he wrapped me in his beast costume. "Come on," he said. "Get into the car. It's freezing out here."

I was warmer in the car, but I couldn't seem to stop shivering. "I thought you gave up and drove home," I said.

"No, we just circled around to see if any lights were on on the other side of your apartment. Then when we got back, we waited and saw Orlop shoving you across the parking lot. I don't know how the police got here though. Unless your mother called them."

As it turned out, it had been my mother. She said she got up when the alarm rang and went looking for me. When she found my hat with the veil on the stairs, she knew I'd been home, and she called the police.

Mother was in worse shape than I was. I felt fine

by the time I got upstairs and was easing away my aches and chill in a nice hot tub of water—a little tired, but fine. Mother was so upset that she had to take a tranquilizer.

My old friend Sergeant Morton arrived. "Well, Kim," he said when I got out of the tub and was sitting in the living room in my bathrobe drinking cocoa, "You don't have to worry about Orlop anymore. Now we've got him on a felony charge for assaulting you, maybe even attempted kidnapping."

"What about the money he took?"

"You mean getting it back? We'll have to see what we can do about that. But you know something funny? We found out he has a mother in jail for pulling the same scam he's been working."

"You're kidding," I said.

"No, the U.S. Postal Inspectors got a case against her on the evidence of a postcard she sent. She was sentenced to five years just because of that one postcard telling a victim where to meet her. No wonder Orlop was uptight about his letter. He probably figured he'd get twice what she got."

"But I thought his mother was dead," I said, remembering how impressed Emma had been because of Orlop's devotion to her memory.

"No, she's very much alive. Tough cookie, Orlop's mama. She's the real brains behind this operation. It seems she conned over fifty people in three different states before she got caught."

"And he went right on doing the same thing?"

168

"Why not? His scam worked pretty well so long as he didn't use the mails. And how was he to know that letter you found was too badly damaged to be any use as evidence?"

"That's what I should have told him," I said. "Now why didn't I think of that?"

"He wouldn't have believed you. You did very well considering the situation you were in," Sergeant Morton comforted me.

In school Monday, Ms. Davis told me Emma wanted to see me. "She's so embarrassed, Kim. I think she wants to apologize to you."

"But she didn't do anything to me."

"Well, if she'd believed you—if *we'd* believed you—maybe you wouldn't have been subjected to such a terrifying experience. I'm as much to blame as Emma with my naive idea that he couldn't be so heartless as to cheat someone who reminded him of his mother."

I told her what I'd learned—that Orlop's mother wasn't dead at all but in jail.

"You mean his saintly mother is a crook?" Ms. Davis began to laugh.

I was glad she could find some humor in it. She was still out a lot of money because of that man.

Emma answered the door when I stopped at the Davises' house after school. She lowered her gaze sheepishly and said, "You're looking at an old fool, Kim."

"No, I'm not, Emma. I'm looking at a great cookie baker and an old friend."

"You're not mad at me?"

"Of course not."

She started to cry and hugged me. "I am an old fool," she said again, "but he acted just like a son to me. And the money—I just wanted so bad for Deirdre to have what she needed for a change. At least she's got something nice happening for her anyway now. No thanks to me."

"What's that?"

"Didn't she tell you . . . ? Come on into the kitchen. I baked you my specialty. It's a seven-layer cake. Takes a whole morning to bake it. That's why I don't make it too often. But everyone always says—"

"Tell me about Ms. Davis, Emma, please," I begged, sitting down at the kitchen table to a glass of milk and the most luscious dessert I've ever eaten in my life.

"You know that professor Deirdre's been writing to? Well, he got some kind of grant. He's going to exchange jobs with an American professor and come here to live for a year. Deirdre will really have a chance to get to know him and then—"

"Wedding bells!" I shouted.

"Well, I don't know about that, but it'll be a treat for her anyway, won't it?" Emma smiled at me.

"Emma," I asked out of sheer curiosity to see

what she would say. "Do you think he's good look-ing?"

"The professor? I wouldn't say so judging by his picture. In fact, I think he's kind of homely myself. But Deirdre's so taken with him she thinks he's nice looking."

Like Morey, I thought. I know he isn't hand-some, and he certainly isn't six feet tall, but even so, this morning my heart actually did a drum roll when I saw him hiking down the hall toward me in school. And it wasn't just from gratitude because he'd done the hero bit for my sake. And it wasn't just a bubbling over of the relief I felt because I don't have to walk around scared anymore. It was— it is—because Morey's such a special guy.

So I guess height isn't that important to me after all. Chalk up one short answer for Kim Terrell. I hope the answers to my other questions don't come as hard, though—and most of all, I hope I never meet another con man in my life.